W. H Rather
Richmond
Texas

If this book falls into your hands read, profit thereby, and return to owner

JIM MILLER'S GIRLS

Jim Miller's Girls

by

LEWIS ERWIN FINNEY

Author of

"DAN'S MINISTRY"

Dallas, Texas
OZARK PUBLISHING CO.

To My Wife,
Who has made my work for
the uplift of men
possible.

CONTENTS

CHAPTER I.

WATER-NYMPHS AT PLAY.

It was early morning, and nature was just waking up to greet the sun, which was threatening to make his appearance over the eastern hilltops. A squirrel was chattering in a pecan-tree, and a mocking-bird, which had been singing to his mate all night, was making the grove across the creek ring with his wondrous melody. More than a mile away, on an eminence to the northwest, the big, deep-toned bell in the tower of the Convent, Villa Maria, was calling the students to early mass, and the distance so softened and mellowed the tones that they fitted harmoniously into the music of the beautiful morning.

The Miller twins had returned from an Eastern college a year before, with "notions in dey haids," as old Rilla, their negro nurse, had declared; and one of these notions had been a bath-house at the big spring, which came boiling up through the white sand on their father's ranch. The water was the same temperature the year around, and the girls had never failed to take their refreshing morning bath, even on the few mornings there had been ice in the creek. They were in the water now, and Rilla was sitting on the steps watching them.

"I declar' ter goodness," Rilla exclaimed, "ef y'all could only see how lubly an' beautiful you are in that cl'ar watah, Y'all would jes' have spells an' spells. Y'all 'minds me o' that paintin' what Mis' Clarissa made an' calls it 'Water-Nimfses.' But, da'lin's, ain't that watah too col'? I knows I'd freeze to def ef I was to stick jes' one foot in dar. Y'all makes me hab a chill jes' a watchin' you."

"Why, Mammy, you make that same speech, and ask that same question, every time we come down here. You have been attending us at our morning baths for nearly a year, and you always ask, 'Ain't it col'?' No, we are used to it, and would not miss it for anything," Jessie replied.

"And you think we are 'perfec'ly lubly and beautiful' in the water, do you, Mammy?" Allie asked.

"Deed I does, baby-chile. That watah is so cl'ar I kin see the seams in y'all's bathin'-suits, and the stitches in yo' hoses. Ef y'all was to drap a pin in thar, I could see it from he-er."

"O then it is the water that is so lovely and beautiful, instead of us, is it?"

"Go 'long now, Miss Allie. You allus is a catchin' up yo' po' black mammy that a way. You knows I neber did see no one in all the whole world as purty as my baby twins. You is jes' fishin' fer a complement, ain't she, Miss Jessie?"

But Jessie's gossamer-clad head was under the water, and she could not hear the question that clearly revealed the black nurse's favorite.

It was an inspiring picture that left nothing wanting to satisfy the heart of artist or poet. The time and the season, the place and its wooded environment, the soft morning light and the chatter of the birds, the two white girls in the water and the black woman on the steps, the fading shadows and the rippling waves, combined to lavish the participants with health and beauty, and leave memories that time could not erase.

An onlooker would have been forced to prophesy that nothing but happiness could ever come to the twins.

As the two young ladies came dripping up the steps to their dressing-rooms, Rilla began again: "I declar' ter goodness, y'all is gettin' purtier every day; and I jes' kain't onderstand how 'tis you is so healthy with all this foolishness o' jumpin' into col' watah in the early mawnin,' when the balance of the while folks is still in they beds."

"Hurry, Mammy. It isn't the plunge that injures one's health; it is being slow about getting into warm garments afterward."

"I is hurryin', Miss Jessie, yessum; but I jes' must talk whilst I works; I kin work better when I is talkin' or singin'. Thar, now. Come along, Miss Allie, honey, an' lemme he'p y'all. Lawdy! but my babies shore is purty, outen the watah as well as in it. Umph! No wonder to me Marse Jim is so foolish about his twins."

The old negro had been in the Miller family all her life, having come with them from Kentucky, and she was so thoroughly devoted to each of them that there was no offense in her familiar talk; indeed, it was the devotion of a voluntary slave who would rather serve them than have a mansion and servants of her own.

As the young ladies left the stone bath-house, the sun was tinting the clouds a beautiful roseate, and the dewdrops were catching the light and reflecting it like myriads of diamonds along the pathway. Again, the distant bell at Villa Maria was intoning its music, the mocking-bird had ceased to sing; but the laughter of children floated across the fields from the near-by town, where they were finding colored eggs in the wet grass, for it was Easter morning.

As they approached the big house that was near enough to the city to be called a suburban residence, a lusty boy, freckled, and almost red-haired, came bounding down the path, barefooted and bare-headed.

"Hello, Jack," called Jessie. "Where are you going with that bathing-suit this time of day?"

"I am going to try your plan of ducking myself every morning to see if it will make me stronger and healthier, as it has you girls."

"Well, I never!" Allie exclaimed. "Only yesterday, you were making fun of us for riding this hobby, and here you are trying to push us off so you can ride yourself!"

"Jes' as I told you," grumbled old Rilla; "it's ketchin'. Why, fust thing we know, little Dixie will be takin' up with it, an' who knows whar it will end! But go on, go on; ef y'all like it, I reckon I kin stand it."

But Jack was running down the path with a jolly laugh that made the glorious morning even brighter as the twins looked after him. He was their only brother, and the baby of the family, and was idolized by every member of the household, as well as by the servants on the ranch.

While they still stood looking after the fast disappearing red-brown head of the boy, a man's voice called from an upper balcony: "Good morning, kids. How's the bathing this morning?"

"Perfectly delightful, Father, dear," replied Jessie.

"Better go and try for yourself," Allie bantered.

"No, thank you, I will take your word for it, babies, I suspect I was bathed too much when I was a child, as I have never liked the water since. Hi, there, Sam!" he broke off, looking toward the barn. "What are you doing?"

"I'se tryin' to ketch this runty pig what you tol' me to 'spose of, Marse Jim."

"Don't you know this is Sunday, you black scamp? I told you to do that yesterday. Just let it alone today, and you had better look spry, or I'll make you go to the ranch, and give Steve your place at the barn."

"Why, Daddy, are you going to have him kill a little pig just because it happens to be smaller than its mates?" asked Allie, in alarm.

"No, baby, I have no idea he will kill it; he will likely sell it to some shiftless negro in town. But I will not allow it to stay on the ranch. This is one place where we really practice the doctrine of the 'survival of the fittest.' But run along now and get ready for breakfast; your mother wants to get an early start, so we can drive over and put some flowers on your grandparents' graves before going to church."

All this time, Rilla had been standing at a respectful distance, muttering to herself: "Now jes' look at them twins! I never did see twins look so much onlike afore. Miss Jessie is 'Night,' and Miss Allie is 'Mornin', when you looks at 'em; but, when you knows 'em, they is both sunshine an' lily-buds, even ef I does lub Miss Jessie the bes'. But whyso shouldn't I, seein' she is the very picter of good ol' Mistus what's a sleepin' in the col', col' ground out yonder in the simitry! They is both angels; that's what they is, and they is too good to be thinkin' o' marryin' the po' white trash what is a comin' to see 'em. I don't know what Marse Jim an' Mis' Mollie can be a thinkin' 'bout to 'low them po' honies to go mixin' up with their onequals. I knows what I knows, umph-umph, an' that Mistah Tallman ain't fitten for Miss Jessie to wipe her little shoes on, ef she on'y knowed it. An' that Mistah Wright makes me think o' them men figgers they got in the winders o' that big store in town. An' him a lettin' on he cum down here to buy hosses! No, sir, he cum to carry Miss Allie off with him, an' he ain't any mo' fitten than Mistah Tallman."

As the twins went up the stairs, Dixie, standing at the top, saw the sunlight fall on Allie's hair as the latter passed the window at the landing, and called: "Wait, Allie! O step back by that window. There. Come up here, Jessie, and look at it. Isn't it the most beautiful hair in the world? The sun makes the bronze coils look almost red. Isn't it beautiful!"

"Yes, Dixie, almost as beautiful as your wealth of jet black," and Jessie caught the dark beauty in her arms and kissed her again and again.

Allie came and joined her in caressing the seventeen-year-old girl. Jessie's hair, between the black and the bronze, struck a happy medium of dark brown. None of the faces were alike; indeed, a stranger would scarcely have discovered a family resemblance. Jessie's eyes were blue, Allie's brown, and Dixie's dark gray. The twins had pink skin; Dixie's was as white as alabaster; not too thin, but giving her mischievous brother an almost irresistible desire to pinch her every time she came within reach.

At the moment the heads were all together, the mother came into the hall. She was a beautiful woman, whose maternity seemed to have given her queenliness without robbing her of youth. She was tall, graceful, and just large enough to indicate superb health and a jolly disposition, with light brown hair, blue eyes, olive complexion, and full, warm lips. She looked more like a sister than the mother of the girls as she kissed each and bade them make haste and come down to breakfast.

Jim Miller was fifty-five years old, the son of an honored minister, who had been chaplain of a Kentucky regiment during the war of the sixties, and who had been killed in battle, while ministering to the wounded, leaving his wife with a small farm, a heavy mortgage, and four children. Jim, then a black-haired, gray-eyed, sturdy boy of fourteen, immediately left school and took charge of things with the avowed purpose of taking care of his mother and three sisters. It was no handicap to him that the Millers had prided themselves on their pluck and indomitable will-power for generations, while the Logans, his mother's people, were among the pioneers that had followed George Rogers Clark to Kentucky, and had gone with him against Old Vincennes. When Jim was twenty-two, his mother had died and his sisters were married; the mortgage had been paid off, and the farm was well stocked with the finest horses in Kentucy. Then, Jim had won and married Mollie Richards, and, after the twins were born, he had moved his family to the great Southwest, where lands were cheap, and interest in fine stock enabled him to make a real success in raising and selling the best. The waters of the Tamalpias Valley had attracted him, and he had bought the ranch that included the over-flowing springs that furnished water for the large town of the same name. Already, the town was becoming a watering-place, and it was also attaining an unenviable reputation as a resort for gamblers and race-track men. There was a good track, and races were held both in the spring and in the fall.

The breakfast-bell rang, and Jim Miller joined his girls in the hall, and went down-stairs with them. He was such a man as any young lady might well be proud to call "Father" in any company; more than six feet tall, his once-black hair now an attractive iron-gray, a closely cropped mustache, shaggy brows, large, thick ears with long lobes, an amused expression lurking about the generous mouth, large hands, which, although rough, were well cared for, a free and easy movement that proclaimed the utter absence of dissipation, and a sparkle in his dark eyes that belongs to the optimist.

As they entered the spacious dining-room, Jack came bounding in, his eyes beaming and his hair tousled, shouting: "Why, girls, that's the most fun I have had since Fido was a pup! I wouldn't take a team of June-bugs for the time I have had this morning. I am going down there every morning after this. Dad, you ought to go along; I just hit it head first, and never was cold after that. Wish I had known how fine it was a long time ago."

"There, now, Son, run along and get ready for breakfast, quickly; you will make us late," admonished Mrs. Miller, and Jack hurried up-stairs, but was down again before they had risen from the table.

It was a beautiful day, and this was a happy family within whose circle love and mutual admiration abounded. The trip to the cemetery was made before going to the church, and the graves of Mrs. Miller's parents were covered with flowers; they had spent their last days with this, their only daughter, and had died just the year before. Then, the family drove to the church of the denomination in which Jim's father had been an honored minister.

Many of the gathering congregation failed to conceal their admiration for the splendid family, and they were outspoken in their praise of the team of big blood-bays "the Colonel," as they called Jim, was driving. Jim seemed to expect and enjoy both kinds of appreciation; he was fond of his family and proud of his horses, and he was never so pleased as when he knew that both were recognized. This pride of fine horses and beautiful women was the Kentucky characteristic that won for him the title of "Colonel."

It was a wonderful congregation that greeted the minister that Easter morning. The women, young and old, came fully up to the reputation of their sex in the South for both beauty and daintiness of attire. The millinery was equal to that worn in the largest cities on the same day, and no one could have guessed that poverty, suffering, disappointment, or heartaches had ever touched a member of this Easter congregation. Even the men were above the average in intelligence, bearing, and signs of health and prosperity. The beautiful stone building was crowded, and chairs were placed in the aisles. The rostrum was banked with white roses, lillies, and carnations, and ferns were on pedestals here and there.

The twins were ushered to the choir, while Dixie and Jack were seated with their parents. An intelligent observer would have noticed the pride showing in Jim Miller's face as the voices of the twins were heard above the others, Jessie singing soprano, and Allie a full, rich alto. Nor was he the only jealous and prejudiced listener. Maury Tallman, the assistant cashier of the First National Bank, was seated in the rear of the church, where he could get an occasional glimpse of Jessie through the billows of hats, and his face glowed with joy as he remembered that she had given him permission to speak to her father.

The minister had said to his wife the day before: "I am sure there is an understanding between Maury Tallman and Jessie Miller, and I do not know whether to be pleased or not. He is of a type that will either make the woman he loves supremely happy, or she will become his slave. He is moral; but, somehow, I do not like the type. I fear he will never be spiritual and temperate enough to make her happy."

"Yes," she had replied; "but he is refined, and has intelligence enough to balance all that. I predict that Mr. Miller will approve of him, and you know his judgment is good and can be relied on. Jessie is so religious that I am sure she will develop his spiritual nature."

But they were not given to gossip, and the subject was dropped.

Across the aisle from the Millers sat Maxwell Wright. While it did not show in his face, he was as much pleased with the appearance and performance of Allie as were the others with Jessie. He was a stranger in Tamalpias, having come there with a stable of race-horses that had won several prizes the fall before, and returning a week before Easter for the ostensible purpose of buying a pacer owned by Jim Miller, but in reality to see the stockman's daughter, Allie. He was non-communicative, but was easily identified as a native of the East by his speech and manner. He was of the type that shrewd men take under suspicion until they learn what the game is, but just the kind that a woman will become unreasonable about when once she has taken a fancy to him.

After the services were concluded, the twins excused themselves to their parents and were soon being driven homeward by their admirers, Mr. Tallman and Mr. Wright. Mrs. Miller invited the young men to stay for the Southern one o'clock dinner, and Maury Tallman accepted the hospitality graciously, and as a matter of course; but Mr. Wright excused himself, saying that he had an engagement. It was evident that he did not consider it conventional to remain. So, having made an engagement with Allie to drive with him that afternoon, he returned to his hotel.

Maury Tallman had heard his mother tell one of her friends that, when she wanted a new bonnet, she always gave her husband a good dinner before mentioning the fact. Remembering this, and deeming it good advice for the matter in hand, he said as they rose from the dinner-table:

"I haven't seen that new colt I have heard so much about, Mr. Miller."

"All right, come with me and I will show you the best piece of horse-flesh for its age, this side Kentucky. I am sure you will agree with me when you see him, if you have studied stock."

"No, sir, I not much judge of horses until I see them on the track."

CHAPTER II.

THE SURVIVAL OF THE FITTEST.

Maury Tallman found it difficult to lead up to the subject he wanted to talk to Jim Miller about, because the latter was so enthusiastic about his stock.

"Just look at that colt! He's only three weeks old, but he is as large and active as most colts twice that age. He is sure to take the prize at the Fair this fall, if he lives to get there. But why shouldn't he? He has a pedigree that runs back at least ten generations on both sides, and all of his ancestors have made good."

"But you sold the last colt by his dam for almost nothing, did you not?"

"Sure. When I found that there was a bad place in the pedigree of her sire, and that she was giving signs of breeding back to the faults of the sire of her sire's dam, I did not have room on this ranch for her. I don't allow any scrubs on this place—horse, cow, chicken, nor even dog. What is the use of breeding scrubs when it does not cost a cent more to keep pure breeds? I have all the runts and defective animals and fowls on this place sold, given away, or killed immediately, lest they perpetuate their imperfections. And I do not like scrub men, either. If there is anything I do admire, it is a manly man, or a womanly woman."

Tallman was somewhat abashed at this last remark; but his ready wit, which had helped him out of many a tight place, came to his relief, and he replied with a laugh: "Well, you are certainly giving the world a fine example of all you have been saying. You have put your theory of the survival of the fittest into practice on your ranch; you are one of the most manly men I ever knew, and your wife and three daughters are truly queenly women."

"Thank you, Tallman, I will agree with you on the first and last propositions; but I can only return the compliment about the other."

This was better than the young man had reckoned, and he hastened to take the advantage it offered.

"By the way, Mr. Miller, I suspect you have noticed that I have been quite attentive to Miss Jessie since she returned from the East. Well, I have her permission to tell you that there is an understanding between us, and that we want your consent to start a home of our own. You are acquainted with my family, you know of my financial standing, and I leave you to judge of my attainments and manhood. I love your daughter very dearly, and will try to make her a good husband if you will allow me to come into the family."

Jim Miller looked far away to the southwest, where a gray cloud was dropping an April shower on Bachelor Peak, and the moisture came into his eyes. He did not answer immediately; but, when he did, he looked the young man full in the eyes and said in a tone that betrayed his deep feeling:

"Yes, I have noticed your attentions, and I have been expecting something like this to happen; but it is mighty hard to think of giving up one of my girls. You can not know what it means until you are called on to do it. I have weighed the matter, and have talked with my wife about it. We believe you to be all right, and that you will cherish our child as your own life. I would not give her to a scrub, nor would I give her to a man that I doubted would make her happy. Take her, but please remember that she is as dear to me as life itself, and I would avenge a wrong done her, under any and all circumstances. Promise me you will never cause her a moment's unnecessary sorrow."

"I thank you for the confidence, and I promise you most solemnly that I will cherish her and make her happy. I have been a little wild, as most men have; but I shall never be untrue to Jessie in the most trivial matter."

"I believe you, my boy. Now run on to her, and let me go and make that nigger water this mare."

Maury found her in a lawn-swing among the shrubbery, and related to her his interview with her father.

"And now you must name the day, and make it right soon, Little Queen; for I should like to take you abroad for the summer."

"Oh! Why, you silly boy, it never could be that soon."

"Why?"

"I must wait for Allie. We can never be

separated until we both marry; it must be a double wedding."

"But what if Maxwell does not come to the point?"

"Never fear. There they go now, and I would wager you a kiss that he proposes before they return, and that she accepts him, too."

"Done! And you might just as well give me the kiss now; for, you see, I win if I lose."

"Rascal! I hadn't thought of that."

"But suppose your father objects?"

"To the kiss!"

"No, to the other son-in-law, teaser."

"Suppose he did; do you think Allie would throw Maxwell over?"

"I hope she would not marry against her father's will."

"So do I; but she is mightily set on marrying him, if he asks her, and he is the kind of man, and she is the kind of woman, that 'laughs at locksmiths.'"

He was silent for a time, and she offered him a penny for his thoughts.

"I was just wondering what we would have done had your father given me a different answer a while ago."

"O, but there was never any question about your being acceptable to my family. It is different with Mr. Wright."

"What does your mother think of him?"

"She has only one serious objection, so far as I know, and that is that he is a Northern man. You know how prejudiced we all are on that line.

Mother says little, but I am sure she would much prefer that we all marry Southern men."

"I am glad I am a Southern man."

"So am I, you great big boy!"

"Are you sorry I am so large, Little Queen?"

"I would not have you otherwise than as you are for anything in the world."

"Not even my mouth, which is so large there had to be a big nose to shade it?"

"If you do not quit slandering my lover, I am going to turn you out."

Just then, Dixie came on them and was about to turn away embarrassed, when Jessie called her, and said:

"Dixie, you are to be the first to share our joy. Father has just given his consent for me to marry Maury. Are you glad to have him for a brother?"

"Yes, if Daddy is willing, it must be all right," and Dixie advanced and gave Tallman her hand.

"You must believe in your father, Dixie," suggested the young man.

"Believe in him! Of course, I do. We all do. Why, Daddy is the best man living, and I know that what he thinks, is all right."

"Well, you can't know how glad I am he thinks me all right. Won't you give your new brother a kiss?"

"No, sir! There will be time enough for that when you are my brother."

"Good for you! I like that, and I like my new sister the better for having such high principles. Stick to them and you will never be sorry."

"Thank you, Mr. Tallman. I think a kiss is too sacred to be given or taken lightly, and I am told that they are more appreciated when they are hard to get; just like the trout in the creek down yonder. Not much is said when one lands a five-pound cat; but a trout half that weight is talked of for a week after the catch."

"What a philosopher my little sister is!"

"Better wait until the wedding is over, Mr. Tallman," and Dixie left the lovers to their planning and went to play with the white rabbits in their clover patch.

When Allie and Maxwell Wright returned from their drive, the sun was gathering the curtains of night about him and taking his evening plunge into a sea of crimson and gold. It was immediately apparent to the couple still in the swing that something very pleasing and important had taken place; and the twins understood each other so well that it was unnecesary for Jessie to explain how matters stood with her and Maury. Again, Mr. Wright was asked to stay to supper, but he politely declined to do so. Not even when Maury told him it would be the occasion of his engagement being announced to the family, would he consent to remain, and he drove off, saying that he would come over later.

In their room that night, the twins discussed their love-affairs with perfect frankness. Both were inclined to the opinion that their father would be slow to give his consent to the marriage of Allie and Mr. Wright, and Jessie, apprehensive of the result, asked Allie what she would do in that event.

"Why, marry him anyway. If Father and Mother do not consent, it will be only because of sectional prejudice, and that is silly, not to say wicked."

"But, Allie, dear, you know so little about him; and how can you be entirely sure he is worthy, and will make you a faithful and loving husband?"

"Just as you are sure of Maury Tallman's virtues. And, more than that, I would marry him if all the world was against us. He asked me what I would do if the family was not willing, and I told him I would go to the smallest island of the sea, or to an adobe house in Mexico with him, and I would!"

"I dislike to hear you talk that way, darling. It is premature even to think such thoughts until he asks Father. When is he going to interview him?"

"I don't know. He dreads it; but I urged him to do it right away. I hope it will be all right, and we can have a double wedding in the church. Wouldn't that be grand!"

"Yes, that is just what Maury and I want. He asked me to name a day in June, and proposed that we go abroad for the summer. You know how much I have wanted to visit Holland and Switzerland. He has been there, and listening to his fine descriptions of the countries and the people has made me very anxious to go."

"Maxwell asked me to name a day in June, too."

"And did he propose a European trip?"

"No, he suggested that we go to some wonderful lakes and streams in Canada, where he has often spent the season fishing and hunting."

"I dislike the thought of giving up our good home, and am distressed with the idea of our being separated when we have always been together; but the thought of life with the man one loves eclipses everything else."

Far into the night, the girls talked. Jessie was the first to fall asleep, and her dreams were all happy. When Allie at last slept, it was the fitful sleeping and waking of one who is troubled; but, finally, her slumber was deep enough for dreams, and she was driving with Maxwell Wright over roads where there were broken bridges, gates to be opened and rough places to impede their progress. At last, it seemed that he gave her the reins and got out to open a gate; the horse was fretful and hard to hold, her hands were tired, and she was about to let the horse get beyond control, when she was awakened by Jessie's warm kisses on her face.

Day after day, for a week, Maxwell Wright put off the interview with Jim Miller. When he did bring himself to speak, he found his fears that there would be objection well founded. Neither the father nor the mother liked the idea of giving their daughter to a man of whom they knew so little, and whose habits and training were so different from hers. If he had talked plainly to Maury Tallman, Jim spoke more freely to Maxwell Wright; and that young man was not open and sincere as Maury had been. His words were smooth; but Jim Miller had studied horses and men all his life to some purpose, and he told him plainly that he believed his habits to be bad, and that he was uneasy about the future happiness of his child if she married him.

The conversation ended by the father saying he would consider the matter and give his answer later. Mrs. Miller told her husband that, while she was not heartily in favor of the young man, she feared Allie was so deeply in love with him that they would find it difficult to break up the affair. She advised him to write to the references Wright had given him, and find out how he stood at home. This he did, and, within a week, he had replies from a banker, a minister, and the mayor of the town. The banker reported him to be a man of means and with business integrity; the minister said that the Wrights were members of his church, and he hoped that Maxwell would soon come into the flock; the mayor was enthusiastic, and warmly recommended him for "anything he wants, up to the Presidency."

In the meantime, Allie had become more infatuated than ever, and was bold to declare her preference before the family, and even to plan for the wedding and her future. Thus it came to pass that the parents gave their consent to the marriage; and they did it heartily, for they were taking a son into the family as well as giving a daughter away. It was characteristic of the family that all followed the example of the parents in making everything pleasant for the newcomer.

It was arranged that the wedding of the twins should take place on the twenty-fourth of June, St. John's Day, in the beautiful stone church, and the engagements were announced at a luncheon the first week in May.

Mr. Wright returned to his home in New York, and Allie wove love into the stitches as she sewed by day, and dreamed of being with her lover in the wilds of Canada, by night. The dreams were seldom troubled now, just an occasional drive when Maxwell would get out and leave her to hold the reins over the fretful horse that always threatened to run away with her; and it was always the same in detail, even to the fact that she would awaken just as she felt she must give up and let the horse run.

Contrary to the adage, nothing came to cause a ripple in the love of Jessie and Maury, not even a lover's quarrel. Old Rilla mentioned it one day, saying:

"Listen to your ol' mammy, honey-chile. Them as has no fuss afore they's married, allus has 'em arterwards. An' it's bes' to have one or two afore the weddin', jes' to see how you is goin' about settlin' 'em at last."

"But, Mammy, we are different from other people; we are never, never going to have a quarrel."

"Humph! Now that jes' sounds like they all says it; 'we is different from other folks, never is gwine to have no quarrelin'.' Den, they goes and quarrels jes' the same, on'y they tries to keep it to theyselves. Lawdy, chile, I seen 'em."

But Jessie kept her own counsel. She knew that her love and lover were different from anything that had ever been, and she was supremely happy.

The announcement of the double wedding created a sensation in social circles, and opinions differed widely concerning the marriage of one of the Miller twins to the stranger from New York. For these were days when prejudices still ran high when any one or anything revived the question of North or South, and Maxwell Wright was from north of the Mason and Dixon line. Old Doctor McConnel was first to mention the matter to Jim Miller, and he did it in a very gentle way.

"I am sorry," he said, "that one of your girls is going away from us, Jim. You will pardon my frankness, but I don't like young Wright. He seems tricky to me, and I am sure he must have sown quite a crop of wild oats."

"I suspect that is true," Jim Miller replied, and the lines tightened about his mouth; "but, then, they all do that these days, and, if a girl waited for a man who had never sowed wild oats, she would go unwed to her grave; isn't it so?"

"Hardly, I believe; but almost so. Very few men keep clean these days. And it is a shame."

"I grant you that, Doctor; but the race seems to get on just the same. You do not think there is anything more than a moral question in it, do you?"

"Yes, we are learning that many things find their origin in the profligate living of our young. But we are just waking up and beginning our investigations along these lines."

They were interrupted just then, and, although Jim Miller determined to ask the Doctor some further questions, time slipped by, and the whole matter was forgotten. In after days he remembered, and that is why this story is written.

CHAPTER III.

TWO JUNE BRIDES.

June is the most trying month in the year in the Southwest. The days are long and sultry; the winds seem to have arranged an armistice after the fierce battle they have been having for three months, and the terrible calm of the mornings, the shimmering heat of noonday, and the heavy, perfume-laden atmosphere of the late evening, drive those citizens who are able to go, to the mountains of the west or the lakes of the north by the middle of the month. The schools are out, the crops are laid by, and those who have supported the churches with their money seem to think that it is no more than right that those who can not take a vacation should attend to the revivals, which, by the way, are always held in midsummer. There is nothing more desolate than such a town emptied of its women and children, leaving the men to attend to what little business there may be going on. However, the approaching wedding of the Miller twins had kept all their friends in Tamalpias, although it was past the middle of the month.

The heat-wave had been long and torrid; but it was broken by a shower on Thursday, and the cloudiness increased until the skies were hidden by a solid canopy of gray all day Sunday. When Rilla called the twins to go for their baths Monday morning, she explained:

"It's jes' too bad! He-er's my sweet babychillern to get married at noon, an' they's not narry star to be seed. I sholy did want my honey-babies to have a putty day to git off in; but it's jes' as liable to rain ag'in as not. Come on, da'lin's, le's go down an' take yo' baths the las' time yo' po' black mammy will ever he'p y'all. O my Gawd, how's I gwine to stan' it?"

"There, there, Mammy, we will come back and bother you lots of times," consoled Allie.

"Taint' no bother. Who said it is bother? Y'all never is been no bother to nobody."

"Stop, Rilla, or you will spoil our wedding-day," warned Jessie, as they walked to the bath-house.

"Yessum, I isn't gwine to say another word ef I kin he'p myself. Go 'long now and take your plunge, an' be happy as that mocking-bird what is singin' in that pecan-tree over there, same as he allus is, jes as ef he was a doin' it fer y'all, special."

The pool was built directly over the springs, and the white sand kept boiling up in a hundred places. The water was about four feet deep, and had just enough mineral in it to make it as clear as crystal. There were several small fish in the pool and one could see them anywhere in the water.

In the early dawn of this June morning, the twins made a romantic picture sporting in the beautiful pool, while the black nurse sat on the steps and talked to herself, as was her habit. The twins had tried to teach her to speak proper English, with the result that she spoke some-

and white myrtle, and wrought out in rosebuds across it were the words: "They twain shall be one flesh." A padded kneeling-board covered with white satin was placed in front of the altar and a bower for the minister behind it. White ribbons were festooned along the ends of the pews on both sides of the aisles; arches, at the ends next to the altar, were hung with gates, on which were ribbons with gold letters reading: "Forsaking all others," and on the other side, to be read as they retired: "Till death do you part."

Preceding the brides, as they came up the east aisle leaning on the arms of their father, flower-girls strewed white flowers, while the pipe-organ filled the building with the slow music of the Lohengrin Wedding-March. Four bridesmaids followed in pairs. Up the west aisle came Maury Tallman, his large face just serious enough to escape criticism, but with the self-reliance and graceful ease for which he was so well known. With him, as his best man, walked Alfred Pryor, a young attorney. Next came Maxwell Wright, with downcast eyes and embarrassed mien, more faultlessly attired than the other bridegroom, but more self-conscious and ill at ease. With him was John Porter Allen, and following them came Stacy Craddock and William Martin.

Never had there been such a wedding in Tamalpias, and it was evident, by the glances in her direction, that the audience knew it had all been planned by the minister's wife, who sat half hidden behind a screen of ferns and plants to the left of the altar. But the multitude did not know that she was thus stationed that she might prompt minister, brides, or bridegrooms in case of embarrasment, or forgetfulness. The ceremony had been most carefully rehearsed; but she had learned from many experiences to be ready for any emergency.

The minister was pale and solemn; but his rich voice was steady and reassuring, and the ceremony was performed without a mistake of any kind. A simple prayer closed the impressive scene. As the prayer was ended, the maids of honor removed the small face-veils worn by the brides, the plaintive notes of the organ took on more volume, and the brides and bridegrooms rose from their knees and turned to retire. The vision of loveliness caused a sigh of admiration to pass over the vast audience, and the party passed through the gate at the west aisle and were soon seated in John Porter Allen's new automobile.

It was after two o'clock when the company entered the spacious dining-room at the Miller home and sat down to the wedding-dinner. The brides were now in gray travelling-dresses. The window-shades were drawn, and candles, from chandelier and stick, suffused the scene with mellow light. Gay talk and mild raillery dispelled the feeling of sadness that would otherwise have settled like a pall over the hearts of the family, and helped to cover the embarrassment of the youngsters that were expected to follow the example of the day in the near future.

At four o'clock, the twins bade the sobbing

servants good-by. Old Rilla cried most piteously, and persisted in kissing the hems of the twins' skirts. The whole party—guests, parents, and all—went to the station, where rice was thrown, and tags were pinned on clothing and baggage, which announced to the world that these were newly-weds. There was much kissing, some tears, promises made to write, and wishes in abundance. As the bell rang, the sun broke through the clouds, and the train pulled out for the East, bearing away happiness that it would never bring back again.

Drury Patterson was at the station, and, when he saw the tears in Dixie's luminous gray eyes, he spoke to her gently, but with such good humor that she was compelled to smile until there were rainbows on her tears. Indeed, Drury seemed to have the happy faculty of making people forget their sorrows in a moment. He had helped many of his school-mates to bear the disappointment of failing to get a letter or pass an examination. He was a real altruist and made others catch the spirit and see matters in their best light. He was a handsome young fellow, whose face called for a second look. There was a breadth of brow, and an expression on the rather square face that betokened intellect and will-power in splendid balance, with hearty good-fellowship and robust health. His figure was strong and manly, and his bearing dignified, yet not stiff. Jim Miller took special notice of him on this occasion, and concluded that he was just the kind of young man with whom he could trust his child. That settled it, and there was never any question raised in the family about Dixie accepting the company of one thus approved by her father.

Marvin Harris, whose father was a retired capitalist, was also at the station, and saw the brightness come into Dixie's eyes at the gentle words of Drury Patterson, and a pang of jealousy went through him. Drury had beaten him in athletic events, scholarship, and morals, and was now making a beginning with a girl he had loved ever since they were children together. Watching his chance, he drew near, and, after a few commonplace remarks, asked Dixie if she would go to the lecture with him the next night.

"I thank you, Marvin; but I have an engagement for the lecture."

"I did not know your parents had given their consent for you to have company."

"They never had before; but I had never asked them."

"O, so you asked them this time, did you?"

"Yes," demurely.

"And who are you going with?"

"Drury Patterson," Dixie answered, simply and frankly.

A gleam came into his eyes as he turned them in Drury's direction, and, if Dixie had been looking, she might have seen the malevolent spirit mirrored there, as he remembered that John Patterson was under heavy financial obligation to his father.

"Well," he said, turning back to the girl, "remember me the next time there is anything doing, Dixie. I would be glad to take you anywhere."

"All right, Marvin. If you ask me some time when I can go, and I have no other engagement, I will accept the invitation with pleasure."

Then, Jim Miller came and gathered his greatly reduced family into the surrey and drove them back to the home that would seem so lonesome for many days to come. Some friends came in to enliven the dull evening, the sun went down in a sea of gorgeous color, and the wedding-day of the Miller twins had gone into history. It remained to be seen whether or not the superstitions of the old negro nurse were portentious.

CHAPTER IV.

THE SUMMER PASSES.

The summer passed by, languidly and slowly. Jim Miller remained at the ranch most of the time; but Mrs. Miller and the two children went to the Ozark Mountains to escape the sultry days of July and August, much to the regret of the young people that could not go away during the heated term. There was no home in the Tamalpias Valley that was so attractive to those who were fortunate enough to count the Millers among their friends.

Letters from the brides were frequent and full of quaint and humorous descriptions of the people and places wherever they went. At first Allie's letters were filled with eulogies of Maxwell Wright and his people, whom they visited on their way North. Then, she told them of the cool mountains and the placid lakes of Ottawa and Ontario, and of the ferns and mosses along the brooks where Maxwell caught trout while she gathered wild flowers. They were camping and fishing, boating and dreaming, in the most romantic way. It seemed impossible that such happiness could ever be marred.

There was always praise for her wonderful husband, who filled her horizon, and satisfied every desire of her feminine heart.

Jessie's first letter was mailed from New York, and was only a newsy note, telling of their time of sailing and where mail was to reach them on the Continent, just a few words about her happiness and the gentle care of her big husband. Then, she wrote from London, and it was plain that, while they were on their honeymoon, they were also touring and sightseeing. It was refreshing to read her original description of London Tower, St. Paul's, St. John's Chapel, where William the Conqueror and his family used to have family prayer, Madame Tussaud's Wax Figures, Hyde Park, Piccadilly, and Westminster Abbey. Then, there were exciting and amusing experiences in shopping, and getting lost in the great crowds.

Dixie read all this with a dreamy look in her eyes, and tried to imagine herself and Drury Patterson on such a trip. She would prefer that to "mooning" in Canada, as Allie was doing. This feeling grew on her as Jessie wrote from gay Paris, and told of the great works of art and the beautiful salons and museums. But it was Holland and Switzerland that made this romantic desire reach the climax of a firm resolve that some day it should all come to pass that she and Drury would visit the islands of Zuyder Zee and watch the inhabitants make Edam cheese, go into the curious little Dutch houses, and lift the lids of the pots to see what they were cooking, look at the Bridal Dresses of Marken, and watch the wooden-shod inhabitants march to church by twos. She did not approve of Allie's idle dreaming; she was not dreaming her life away, but rather having visions of happiness and activity yet to come.

Thus the summer passed; Allie dreaming and writing of her amorous husband, Jessie traveling in Europe and evidently enjoying her mate as well as Allie, but saying little about it, Dixie resting in the Ozarks and having visions of the time when Drury would be a great surgeon and they would tour the world together, then settle down to be a blessing to suffering humanity. Of course, they were only children now; but they would be grown in three or four years, and they were going to be true to each other forever.

Meanwhile Jack was building muscle by climbing the mountains and hunting with an old mountaineer, named Sol Trimble, who claimed to be the ugliest man in the world. His skin was a reddish purple, and hung in folds and wrinkles on his face and neck, his hair was a muddy yellow, and his eyes were so nearly white that one could not see the iris at first glance. He went clean-shaven, so that people could appreciate his claim, which was never challenged. He made up for his external hideousness, however, by having a sunny disposition and a ready wit, which drew around him a host of friends, including summer boarders as well as native mountaineers. Under his guidance, Jack soon became an expert rifle shot, and threatened to know the mountain-trails and the haunts of game as well as "Old Man Sol."

"By crakies!" exclaimed the latter, one day near the close of the summer, "ef you'll come up here ag'in next year, we'll fix up and take a trip over in Baxter and Searcy Counties, an' ef I don't show you sumpin' in the way of big game, fishing, and findin' bee-trees, I'll let my whiskers grow out ag'in and give up the champeenship fer ugliness to that pie-faced feller from Saint Looey that has allus got a look like he had just heard that his mother-in-law was a-coming to visit him. You shore must fetch him with you ag'in Mis' Miller; he's the finest chap as ever grew outside o' Arkansaw."

Jack was not only popular with the old hunter; but he was a favorite with men and women, and many mothers pointed him out as an example and ideal for their sons.

The resort at which they stayed was the highest point in the Ozarks near a railroad. Indeed, the hotels and cottages were built on a high ridge through which a long tunnel had been made for the railroad to cross the crest of the mountains. To the south could be seen beautiful Blue Canon, where the trains puffed and snorted as they wound in and out through the cuts and over the high bridges, past cliffs and gulches that made the passengers crane their necks from the windows to take in the beautiful scenery. It was one of Dixie's diversions to sit on a large rock high over the tunnel and watch the steam rise from the distant train, then strain her ears to catch the echoes of the shrill whistle some moments later; or to sit there at night, and trace the progress of the "Night Express" as the electric headlight shot its rays into the darkness, reminding her of the tail of a comet. At last, there would be the deafening puffing of the monster engines, then the trembling of the earth, as the train entered the tunnel. Then she would get up and climb quickly to the top of the ridge in time to see the lights emerge from the other end of the tunnel, and hear the grinding of the wheels as the train came to a stop at the little station for a few moments, and then sped like a specter of the night through the valley to the north, the whistle screeching alarms that echoed and re-echoed until they died away in harmony with the medley of the crickets and katydids.

When summer was ended, and they returned to Tamalpias with the priceless treasure of health and vigor, Jim Miller saw at a glance that Dixie was no longer a child, but that she was a most beautiful young lady, and the thought came to him, accompanied by a keen pain, that she would soon slip out of his home to make one of her own.

Drury Patterson was also at the station, and there was a sparkle in his eye and a tinge of red on his cheek as he caught sight of the beautiful young woman whose two or three letters were in his pocket very near to his heart. Whether it was accident or intention, he found himself suddenly displaced, and he saw Marvin Harris take Dixie's umbrella, lift her into his waiting carriage, and drive her away without even waiting for her to speak to the few friends that were there. Jim Miller saw the episode and did not know whether to be displeased or amused; but, seeing Drury's smiling face as he came to welcome Mrs. Miller and Jack, he decided that, after all, it was only a schoolboy affair, and he dismissed it from his mind.

But Marvin Harris was taking all the advantage his little coup afforded him. His plan had succeeded splendidly, and he was not slow to improve his opportunity. He soon brought his horse to a walk and began to talk seriously.

"This has been a long, dreary summer, Dixie. I have been miserably lonesome, and I can not bring myself to think of the winter with you gone from town. I have always been fond of you; but this absence has revealed to me what life would be without you, and I am taking this opportunity to tell you of my love, because you are to leave for college next week. I may not get another chance. Tell me that you care just a little for me, Dixie."

"I am sorry you have said this, Marvin; for I am sure I can not discuss the matter now. My preparation for life and other matters make it out of the question for me seriously to consider such a proposition."

"Come now, Dixie, you can't put me off like that. I know that your soul has awakened, and that the question of marrying is not altogether hateful to you. Is there any one else? Wouldn't you discuss this question with Drury? Ah, I see the blushes come to your cheeks. And I have suspected that he was writing to you while you were gone. But I want to tell you now that you shall never marry that son of a low-down drunkard if I can prevent it, and I think I can."

"Marvin, I did not suspect you were so jealous, nor that you would taunt me in this way. And I remind you that I have a father who is able to advise and protect me at all times without your interference or assistance."

"Yes, I am jealous, and I don't care who knows it. I have loved you ever since you were a little girl, and, when I used to call you my little sweetheart, you did not resent it; and, now that you are a stunningly beautiful young lady, you must consider my claims to a place in your heart. Don't turn from me like that. You are to be my wife some day. Come, give me a smile at least."

Dixie was saved further embarrassment by their arrival at home, and the pleasant surprise of some waiting friends, who had come to welcome them. It was a happy occasion, except that the family missed the twins more than ever. There were letters from Maury and Jessie, saying that they would be at home within two weeks. There was one letter from Allie, telling them that she was ill at her new home in New York, but that her physician was hopeful, and that she expected to be well enough to come to them at Christmas.

The following week was a round of receptions and parties in honor of returning tourists and departing students. The Miller home was the scene of one of the gayest of all these entertainments Thursday night, when Dixie was given a party to which all her old schoolmates came that they might bid her farewell, as she would leave the following Monday for college. So many were the claims on her time that Drury did not get to see her alone long enough to tell her the message that burned in his breast; but she promised him a few hours on Sunday afternoon. The promise was not given too soon, for Marvin came to her a few minutes later, and asked the privilege of calling at that very time. When she told him she had an engagement, he became furious, and grasped her arm until the tears came to her eyes, as he almost hissed:

"You had better remember what I told you about that low-born scamp. He is not fit to look at you, much less to marry you."

"Low-born or not, he is a gentleman, and I am sure he would not offer both insult and injury to a girl, as you are doing. I am ashamed of you!"

"Forgive me if I have seemed to offer you either, Dixie. It is only my love for you that makes me so intense."

"It is certainly a queer way to show love."

"When you know what love is, you will think better of me. I want you to promise to write to me sometimes."

"I really can not do that, as I do not know how much liberty and time I will have for correspondence. If you mean to ask me to take up a sentimental correspondence with you, I answer you frankly that I can't do that under any circumstances."

"Why?"

"For reasons of my own."

"Can you tell me truthfully that you will not

undertake such correspondence with Drury Patterson?"

"Mr. Harris, what right have you to institute an inquisition into what I shall or shall not do? I resent your impudence, and I will thank you to cease referring to Drury Patterson in this way. I should dislike to have to call my father to my defense."

"Mr. Harris! Well. I like that. Here I have known you since you were a baby; we have played together all our lives, and you call me Mr. Harris! Come now, Dixie. this won't do; we must be friends."

"You are five years older than I, and your conduct demands that I treat you as a mere acquaintance, so I shall continue to refer to you in a conventional way."

"Very well, Dixie, but remember the day will come when you will call me by a more familiar name or wish that you could."

"What do you mean?"

"I mean that you are either to be my wife, or we are to be the worst enemies in the world. Love like mine must either be requited, or it turns to implacable hatred."

There was such a determined look in his eyes that Dixie went pale and turned sick at heart. Visions of harm to herself, or worse, to Drury, flitted before her, and he saw it and smiled. As he turned away, he bent over her and said in a low, thrilling voice:

"Your happiness and mine are in your own hand; and I swear to you that we are to be happy or miserable together."

CHAPTER V.

GATHERING CLOUDS.

It was Christmastide, and Dixie was at home for the holidays. The day before Christmas, she was at Jessie's new home, a California cottage that had been built for them while they were in Europe, and was listening to her sister's graphic accounts of the wonderland of the Old World. It was almost like a real trip to hear Jessie recount the things she had seen and the incidents along the way. Finally, the conversation turned to Allie.

"I am so sorry Allie could not come this Christmas," Dixie was saying. "It seems an age since she went away. And to see you here without her makes her absence more keenly realized."

"Yes, Dixie; but you can scarcely feel as I do about it, because I was never away from her before. While I was abroad, the excitement and the new experience of Maury's company kept me busy; but since coming home, I have been so lonesome without her, I am really nervous. And I am alarmed about her health. She has always been the stronger of the two, and I was sure she would be benefited by the summer in Canada; but her illness seems to be serious. I wish she could come home and let Dr. McConnell treat her; I am sure he could cure her."

"O, I am sure she is not very ill. She wrote Mother this week that she was able to ride out each day, but that she did not feel equal to the long ride on the cars. I hope she will be all right soon, and she is coming as soon as she can stand the trip."

Their conversation was interrupted by the arrival of Maury. Dixie caught her breath as she saw his happy face wreathed in a glorious smile as he caught Jessie in his strong arms and kissed her face and her hair. He was the very picture of manhood, and his happiness made him as handsome as Dixie had dreamed Drury Patterson would be, when he attained perfect manhood.

"Excuse me, dear, I must give the workmen some instructions about that garage. Here is a letter that you will want to read while I am out," and he kissed her again, and handed Jessie a letter.

"From Allie!"

As she read, her face clouded, and her breath came in gasps.

"What is it, Sister?" Dixie asked.

"Oh, she is worse, and she fears an operation will have to be performed before she will ever get well. I do wish she was at home. I am going to write her at once to come home and let us nurse her, and Dr. McConnell will cure her, I am sure."

Every member of the Miller family believed in Dr. McConnell. The fact that he was on his way to the bedside of a sick one gave hope and cheer, and even the negroes on the ranch began to improve as soon as they saw the Doctor's gray horse being hitched in front of their doors. Indeed, the old physician had treated the family for so many years that he knew their predispositions and temperaments better than they knew them themselves, and that is no mean advantage in medical science.

The holidays passed swiftly for Dixie. She went to several "parties," as the social gatherings in that section are called, and was always a favorite with both girls and boys. Drury Patterson had not returned from school, and Marvin Harris took advantage of that fact to impose his company on Dixie as much as he dared. He was more gentle and considerate than he had been before. Drury's name was not mentioned between them until the day Dixie started back to college, when Marvin asked,

"I suppose you know that Drury Patterson's father had delirium tremens yesterday, and is almost dead?"

"No, I had not heard that. I am sorry, and hope he will recover and give up his habit."

"He may recover, but he will never give up his drink. And his son will most surely follow in his tracks. I have been reading some articles on heredity, and all the specialists say that a drunkard imparts his appetite for strong drink to his children. It would not surprise me to hear that Drury has fallen, and, when he does, he will go quick; they always do."

"Don't you think you are uncharitable to suppose that Drury has no will-power of his own? I do not believe for a moment that he will ever take to drink."

"No, you are prejudiced in his favor; but time

will tell." There was that in his voice and manner that told plainly that he hoped his implied prophecy would come true; also, he revealed his old jealousy, and this stung Dixie into silence.

When she was alone on the train, there came to her a dread fear that all he had said might be true. She had read something like that herself, and she determined to make investigation along that line. The newsboy, with his armful of magazines, suggested that perhaps she could find something in a current publication that would throw light on this terrible problem. Nor was she disappointed. The first magazine she opened had an article entitled "Is Alcoholism Hereditary?" The author was a noted physician, and he quoted from many authorities to prove his contention, and finally summed the matter up with this startling declaration:

"It is a fact in science that the families of drunkards do not live beyond the fourth generation. In the first generation, there is found moral depravity and alcoholic excess; in the second generation, drunkenness and maniacal outbursts, delirium tremens; in the third generation, melancholia and impulsive ideas, especially bloodthirst and murder; in the fourth generation, the imbecile and the idiot appear, and the family becomes extinct."

The book fell from her hand and she shook as with an ague. No greater shock could have come to a young woman than this. She looked about, but there was no one on the car that she knew. She almost screamed out with the pain that gnawed at her heart. Drury Patterson was the child of a drunkard; he was doomed to become a victim of this terrible habit. But he was now a grown man, and the appetite had not developed in him. Surely, there was a mistake, or he was the exception that proved the rule. Yes, that must be it. She had heard Doctor McConnell say something like that, and she comforted herself with the thought. Two men seated in front of her were talking loudly, and, now, she heard one of them say, very distinctly:

"I do not agree with you at all. In my experience as a physician, I find that more harm has been done by the articles printed in the magazines than there has been good accomplished. I grant you that some of the articles are written by competent men, and some of them, indeed many of them, are correct. But the general public is not able to interpret them, and opinions and prejudices are formed that are unjust and incorrect. Take, for instance, the current articles on tuberculosis; all good, but only the alphabet given the public, and the readers think they are graduates, and will never need the advice of a competent doctor on the subject."

"Well, I am not a doctor, but I do believe that our hope lies in giving publicity to the facts. At least, the intelligent people will give heed, and they will be the first to seek further help from you doctors."

"But, while that is true, young people are reading these articles, and are becoming needlessly alarmed in regard to things of which they can know little or nothing."

Dixie wanted to hear more, but at this point the two men had reached their destination, and she was left to the conflict of her fears, and her hope that Drury was a notable exception to the rule of heredity. She realized now that she loved him with all her heart, and that heart kept saying:

"He is all right; he is different from other men; he surpasses others in will-power, and will never fall like a weakling. No, Drury will never drink; he loves me too well to do anything like that. I wish Marvin had not told me all that. His father is such a paragon of morality and temperance in all things that he delighted to have me compare him and Mr. Patterson. But one would think Drury the son of such a man as Mr. Harris, rather than of John Patterson, and Marvin is scarcely a duplicate of the older Harris. I just know it is all a mistake. But I am going to write to Drury and ask him to shun temptation if it ever comes his way."

On and on, in the way of the love-lorn maiden, she communed with her heart until the train reached the college town of Traskwood.

When he had told her of Mr. Patterson's attack of delirium tremens, Marvin Harris had noticed the sudden paling of Dixie's face, and, that very night, he wrote a dissolute friend, who was at the State University, and told him he wanted him to cultivate Drury Patterson, and "show him a good time," but never to mention that it was at his request. Tom Murdock lost no time in hunting up Drury and getting a lot of the "bunch" to try to lure him out for "a night off."

It is quite possible that Drury would have joined them in what he supposed was an innocent "lark" had he not received an extraordinary letter from Dixie, in which she requested him to beware of getting in the way of temptation that might be hard to resist. She was very plain, and told him that he had a harder battle to fight than if his father was a temperate man; and it must be set down to Drury's credit that he did not resent her plain words, but rather appreciated them. Later on, however, he did go with the "fellows" on a Saturday trip to the Coast, and he found that they were all wild and dissipated. But he found the taste, and even the smell, of drink so obnoxious that it was no temptation to him. The worst task was to resist doing that which was really distasteful to keep from offending his comrades. But he was firm, and told them it was both a physical and a moral question with him. Nor could he understand why he did not like the drink, when his father used it, and he had been fed "toddy" in babyhood.

In the meantime letters brought the news that Allie was worse and that the attending physician was insisting on an immediate operation. Jessie went East to be with her and, in March the parents followed, in answer to a telegram, and they took Dr. McConnell with them.

Mrs. Miller could not repress the sobs as she saw the colorless face of her child among the pillows. All she had written about the luxury that surrounded her had failed to prepare them for what they beheld. Everything that could delight the eye or please the senses was made to contribute to the loveliness of Maxwell Wright's palatial residence. Tapestries and hangings, statuary and art, fountains and flowers. musical instruments and pets, landscape and architecture, were the realized dream of artist and artisan. Servants were at every turn, and two trained nurses were in attendance on the invalid. Mr. Wright's parents were the dearest couple the Millers had ever met, and the pain in Jim Miller's heart was somewhat eased at this revelation of the care and luxury that surrounded his child.

After consultation it was decided that the patient should have two weeks of special treatment before the operation should be attempted. The longer the Millers stayed, the better they liked their daughter's relatives. They were leading people in the town, and were universally liked, the elder Mr. Wright being a popular lawyer, and his wife a noted church-worker and director of several charities. Maxwell had been wild, but had settled into a very sedate life since his marriage, and was proving his ability as a business man and a money-maker.

Mrs. Wright gave one the impression that she had a great sorrow in her life, and, within a week, she took Mrs. Miller into her confidence and told her the story:

"Mr. Wright was at his office late one night and walked home. It was winter, and a heavy snow was on the ground. As he passed a corner store, three blocks from our home, he saw a little girl leaning against the wall, and she was sobbing as she shivered in the cold. He asked her why she did not run home, and she said she had no home. In reply to his questions, she told him that her parents were both dead and she had been left in the town by a women with whom she had lived for two years. He brought her home, dirty, ragged, cold, and nearly sick. But, when she was well, and I had gotten her skin healed and her hair brushed she was the prettiest child I have ever seen. She was about eleven years old then, and she quickly grew into our hearts and we into hers. I had but the one child, and this girl seemed to fill a place in my life that had been empty. We sent her to school, and she grew to womanhood under our care. Then, an awful day came: she met a woman on the street, and was recognized. The woman was her sister, whom she had never seen. She proved her relationship. Surely blood is thicker than water, and it will tell. Almost before we knew it, my child had learned the ways of her wicked sister.

"One day, while I was packing her clothes in a trunk, she came in and sat on the arm of the rocker in which Mr. Wright sat, put her arm around his neck, and sobbed out: 'Papa, I wish I was dead!'

"He replied: 'I do too, Mollie.'

"I really wish she had died the night he found her. Our hearts were broken; but we could do nothing except give her over to the sister, who had ruined her. We told her that if we could ever help her to call on us and we would do what we could. Five years passed by. Then, a telegram came, asking us to come to her. We did not get there before she died. Oh, it was in a jail, and she lies buried in a grave of shame—shame into which she was sold by her own sister."

It is needless to say that the story melted the heart of the woman whose child lay in the next room so near to death's door; and only God knows how much this grief softened the hearts of the Millers toward the Wrights in the coming months and years. Knowledge of another's sorrow gives us charity for their faults, and it is grief that makes all mankind kin.

It was the middle of April when Allie was removed to the sanitarium for the crucial ordeal that was ultimately to mean life or death for her. The snows of winer had given way to the breath of spring, and the fragrance of lilacs and cherry-blossoms filled the air. Life was abounding everywhere, and all were full of hope that the invalid would recover in a very short time. Dr. McConnell said little, but that little kept the parents hoping and praying that their child would survive and fully recover.

CHAPTER VI.

IN THE VALLEY OF SHADOWS.

If it was not for the Valley of Shadows, there would be no tragedies in life. We could have poetry and art without the Valley of Shadows; but drama and tragedy would be insipid, indeed, without exquisite pain and heroic suffering. Men may not believe in vicarious suffering, but that is because they have not stopped to analyze the real tragedies of life. And where will you find such a garden of tragedies as under the somber roof of a great hospital? If the angels that hover over the unconscious forms, and peep over the shoulders of nurse and surgeon, could write what they see and hear, their stories would break the heart of every reader, and the world would be the better for the sympathies thus awakened. Nor is it any sordid purpose that records these lines as we follow one of the Miller twins down into the Valley.

One after another, the tables were wheeled into the mysterious room, where the great surgeon was performing real miracles of healing. Below, in the beautiful parlor, six people sat in silence, save that there escaped a few whispered words from the two elderly women, an occasional groan from one of the three men, and a smothered sob from Jessie. Maxwell sat like a statue, but one could see he was suffering keenly. Jessie watched the clock on the ornamental brick mantel, and, when it marked eleven, her sobs increased; that was the hour set for the tragedy on the fourth floor. Maxwell rose and walked out of the room to the corridor, and his father followed him; Jim Miller sat with his face in his hands, and mastered his grief only for the sake of the wife of his youth, who was really under better self-control than any other member of the sad company.

It was high noon when a nurse entered the parlor and told them the Valley had been passed, and that they could take a peep at the patient through the open door of the room to which she had been removed on the second floor. Here, they found the old Doctor in close attendance, and a special nurse, who had been detailed for service during the day. Allie's limp form lay on the white bed, and it would be two or three hours before she recovered consciousness, and would be entirely out of the Valley; but Dr. McConnell whispered to Jim that the operation had been successful, and that he had never seen a finer surgeon than Dr. Duncan. He added, however, that it would be several days before definite promise of the future could be made.

Late in the afternoon, the party visited the sick-room, and the meeting between the twins was pathetic in the extreme, while that between husband and wife was so sublime that the Millers had final proof of the love of both. Dr McConnell said later that he had never s more tender and lovable husband in his life the visit seemed to prove a tonic to the patie..

But days multiplied into weeks before the

physicians would consent for Allie to undertake the trip to the old home, and it was the last of May when the party arrived at Tamalpias, and once more the whole family was under the Miller roof at the same time. Old Rilla was always on hand, and was jealous of the trained nurse that had come with them; she know she could take better care of her "baby-chile" than any white nurse could. Allie improved very slowly, and it was decided to take her to Colorado for the summer, and Rilla was in the heights of ecstasy when told that she was to go with them to nurse the invalid.

"Thar, now," she said, "I knowed that white nuss doan know how ter nuss my angel-twin; do she, honey? I's jes' gwin ter git you well in a minit, I is. I's gwine ter git some yarbs, and make some tea, and you shore is gwine ter be well right off."

Maxwell's attention was unceasing and tender. He seemed to realize that Allie was not to stay with him long, and he made the most of her company. She was uncomplaining and patient at all times, and showed more consideration for the comfort and pleasure of others than she had ever done before. She soon discovered the status of affairs between Dixie and Drury, and succeeded in winning the confidence of both. She laughed at Dixie's fears until Dixie felt that she had wronged Drury even to think of such a thing as his ever yielding to an appetite for strong drink, if he should discover that he had one.

It was while they were sitting on a large rock,

gazing at the mountain-peaks of the Great Divide, that Allie told Maxwell of her dreams. She was leaning against him, and pulled the great shawl closer about her as she said:

"Darling, I never did tell you about the dreams I had before we were married. I dreamed so often that we were driving, and that you got out to open a gate or something; the horse became fretful and ran away with me, and I always awoke just as the horse was getting entirely beyond my control. And, the day of the operation, as I went under the influence of the anesthetic, I dreamed it all over again just the same way, and I became conscious again just as the horse seemed to be plunging off a high precipice."

"I am so glad you returned to me before the horse did plunge; and I wish you could know how it hurt me that I could not suffer for you, my precious wife. I never realized before what suffering is; I have always been well, and I have never seen suffering; but I did suffer with you. I do so much want you to get well and let me make your life a round of happiness. My love has been a selfish one; now, it is your pleasure I shall seek."

"How you make me want to get well! I will if I can; but I feel my strength slipping from me, and I can not get the inspiration of hope that I am going to get well, at all. Really, I feel sometimes that I shall not be with you much longer, my sweet boy. There, don't let those tears fall that way. I haven't given up, and I shall try harder after this little talk; but, if I do go, I want

"The first time I saw them," said Maxwell, "was at the races two years ago, and I fell in love with Allie that very day. The more I knew the family, the more I felt my own unfitness to marry her. I was pretty wild, Tallman, and I had flirted with women everywhere. I had had several romantic affairs, and thought I was in love two or three times; but what rot! Now, if I should lose her, I am sure I would never look at a women again."

"Well, I was reared with them, and I always knew that Jim Miller was giving to the world a very fine family; but I did not think of loving Jessie until she came back from college just the same sweet, heart-free girl she went away. She tells me that neither of them ever had a love-affair until they met us. We are very fortunate men, Wright. I only wish I was more worthy of the love of such a pure woman. Like you, I sowed my wild oats, and I detest myself when I think of the low standards I used to have. Marriage makes such a difference in a man's thinking; I really believe there ought to be some kind of legislation to check the wildness of young men. I do not know what it ought to be; but I am sure it is not right to allow a pure young woman to meet a foul, dissolute young man at the altar, when he would not marry her if she was half as unfit as he. I hope some reformer will arise to work a social revolution before I have a daughter to give away."

"That is what is killing me. I not only stand a fair chance to lose my wife, but Dr. Duncan told me that she will never be a mother, even if she gets well. The operation destroyed all hope of that. I cannot see why a woman brought up as she was, and with the superb health she had when we were married, should become such an invalid. I have given her every care, and it must be as our minister says, it is the curse of God on womankind. If that is it, I am frank to say that I think it an unjust affliction of innocent persons."

"I would not be hasty in saying that; we are learning that many things that have been charged up to the arbitrary will of the Creator are only the natural result of the violation of some of the laws of Nature. It is a Chinese puzzle; but the solution will be known some of these days, and it may be that we shall find the cause of such suffering nearer home."

Maury spoke at random; however, he was nearer the truth than either of them knew. He was destined to know the awful facts in the near future, for the question was to come home to him in a way it had not come to Maxwell.

Women take such things more as a matter-of-course, and without questionings and surmises. So Allie suffered on, and found a little envy growing up in her heart as she watched the dainty work in the hands of her sister growing into a wardrobe of doll-like proportions.

Maury returned to Tamalpias after four weeks and left Jessie to spend the remainder of the heated term with Maxwell and Allie. When he reached home, there were letters for him that made it probable he would accept a position with a bank at Sharman, a new town near the border of Mexico. He discussed the matter with Jim Miller, and the latter advised him to accept it, as the opportunity was great for him to make more money and have a better position than the one he then held. It was hard for Mrs. Miller to consent to the arrangement, as it would take the other twin away from home; however, she saw the wisdom of the change and determined to make the best of it.

Thus it happened that, by the time Jessie returned home, everything was ready for the move, and she had only a few days with her mother before going to make a really new home among strangers. Her mother promised to come to her during the winter, and that made it easier for both of them.

Maxwell's business interests demanded his attention at home, so he and Allie took up their journey after a visit of two weeks at Tamalpias. Old Dr. McConnell shook his head when Jim Miller asked him what he thought of Allie's prospects of being strong again.

"I fear she will never be well again, Jim. If she had improved more this summer, I would be more hopeful; but it now looks like invalidism for life. Another operation may be necessary; but I hope not; it is a stubborn case, and one that is hard to forecast."

So it was with heavy hearts that they bade Allie good-by and saw her leave the scenes of her happy childhood.

CHAPTER VII.

DIXIE MILLER.

Dixie Miller had begun to realize that "Life is real, life is earnest," for the hard work of the school-year, added to her uneasiness about Allie, and her hopes and fears about Drury Patterson, had quickly developed her into a serious young lady. Her parents were awed at the change in her looks and her demeanor, and the thoughtful father spoke to her very gently about it.

"I am afraid, Dixie," he said, "that you are taking things too seriously. Perhaps you are working too hard at school?"

"No, Father, I have not worked harder than others; indeed, not as hard as some have had to work to keep up. But I can not help worrying about Allie. I am going to tell you my secret, Daddy: I care a great deal for Drury Patterson, and I am told that his father had a severe attack of delirium tremens last winter. I haven't told another living soul about it; but I have wanted to talk to you, and ask if you think Drury will ever take up the habit?"

Jim looked down into the face of his child for some time before answering her question. There was admiration, astonishment, pride, and love mingled in his look. His children had always been frank with him, with the possible exception of Allie, and this supreme confidence and candor in his youngest daughter stirred him deeply. He seldom yielded to his emotions; but, now, he

and I have it in mind to help him get his education if he needs my help."

The caress the daughter gave her father fully paid him for his promise and his kindly words. Both remembered this conversation in after years, and the father came to appreciate the wisdom of his daughter even more than he did this summer day on the lawn at Tamalpias.

As they rose to return to the house, both were surprised to see Drury enter the gate; for he was supposed to have accepted a position for the summer in the city where the University was located and it had not been his intention to come home. However John Patterson had reached that point in his inebriacy that he thought it reflected on him for Drury to remain away during the summer and he had ordered him to come home.

This was about the time Maxwell and Allie had left for the mountains of Colorado, and the Harris family had already left for the North; so that, owing to the fact that Mrs. Miller was not going away for the summer, Dixie and Drury saw much of each other without the interference of the jealous rival. Drury told her of his trip to the Coast, and of his experience with the jolly crowd. This reassured Dixie, and she freely expressed her faith in his manhood and his determination never to touch the fiery liquid that had been his father's undoing.

With the relief of Allie's improvement, and the end of her anxiety about Drury's future, the rest began to bring the health-bloom back to

Dixie's pale cheeks. Then, too she took up the twins' habit of going to the pool for a plunge every morning; and, if the twins had been beautiful she was more so. Even Jack became enthusiastic about her and it was a wonder she did not become vain over the attention she received everywhere she went. However she was too sensible to have her head turned by the fact that she had a beautiful face, for she had heard Dr. Barnes preach on "Solomon's Quest of the Chief Good," and she remembered that one of his main points was "The Vanity of All Personal Beauty," which he said, could be snatched away by sickness, sorrow, or an accident.

When Marvin Harris came home, two weeks before she returned to school, he did not share her opinion on that matter; and he was more infatuated than ever. Drury had been content to sit in mute worship of the pure character that he knew was resident in this beautiful house. But not so Marvin Harris. His eyes ravished her face and form, and he told her of her charms in such eloquent terms that a less sensible girl would have been won by his ardent admiration. Even she blushed as she realized woman-like, that such praise and attention were not altogether distasteful. However, it is the ardent, aggressive lover that is lacking in tact. He always spoiled his compliment by some slighting reference to his rival.

Dixie assumed an attitude of placid indifference when Marvin referred to Drury, and refused to be drawn into any discussion regarding him or his family, to such purpose that Marvin ceased to annoy her in that way. Nevertheless, he was by no means satisfied to let it go at that. He knew that Mr. Patterson would not be able to send Drury back to the University without borrowing money, and he was sure that his father would be appealed to in the matter. Nor was he mistaken. He was in his father's office when John Patterson came on that very errand, and, while they were talking, he wrote a note and passed it to his father, asking him not to lend any more money on collateral that was even now covered by amounts approaching its real value. The note was opportune, and Mr. Harris kindly, but firmly, told his client that he could not accommodate him further. It was a hard blow, and John Patterson begged and made promises, to no purpose; for he had promised before, and had always broken his word at the first temptation.

Drury said not a word regarding his keen disappointment. Not even to his mother, nor to Dixie, did he utter a word of complain. He merely set about to find employment, and, failing in town, he applied to Jim Miller for a place on the ranch.

"Why," replied Jim, "I thought you were going back to the University."

"I was; but my father can not spare the money, and I will have to work this year and make enough to go to school next year."

"So you are not going to give up the ambition to get an education, then!"

"Never, sir. It will take longer; but I suspect I will appreciate it the more."

"Give me your hand, son. That is the stuff men are made of. You will succeed in life, and I want to help you. I will make you a proposition: I will loan you one thousand dollars, and you can pay me when you are through school and getting an income of two thousand a year."

"But, Mr. Miller, I have no way of securing you for such a loan."

"I want no other security than your word, my boy. I have watched you for years, and I believe in you thoroughly. I only exact one condition: you are to return to me the unexpended balance that may be on hand if you ever take a drink of intoxicating liquor, and our friendship will then be at an end."

"I gladly subscribe to the condition, yet I hesitate to accept such a large loan when it will take so long to repay it."

"You need not hesitate a moment; it is my proposition and I want you to accept it in the spirit in which it is offered. Of course, you understand that none of the money is to be diverted to any other purpose, and it would be just as well to keep the matter confidential between us."

"Before I accept it, I have a confession to make to you, Mr. Miller. There is a mutual understanding between me and Dixie. I do not ask you for her hand, because that is a matter out of the question until I have an education and an income that will support her as your daughter ought to be supported. But I think it is time you knew that I love her, and I could not accept your proffered help without knowing that you have no objection to our correspondence."

"There now, that is the sort I took you to be. I admire your frankness, and I hope the time will never come when you will not be straightforward like that. I am glad you see that you must not think of marriage until you are settled and have an income on which to support a wife. Three years is quite a while, and, if you still feel like this at the end of that time, I want you to tell me so. For the present, you must give yourself to hard work; and I would advise you to concentrate on the study of medicine if you are settled in making that your profession."

"I can not thank you enough, Mr. Miller, for your great kindness to me. I shall try to prove my gratitude by making a place for myself in the profession, of which you shall not be ashamed. I am going to the top if I can get there."

"God bless you, my boy," and the two men shook hands and separated.

Marvin Harris was chagrined when he found that Drury was going to school again. Although he tried every way to find out where he got the money, it remained a mystery to him and other curious people for many years. Dixie surmised what had happened because of the remark her father had made, to her, although the subject was not mentioned between them.

September found both students back at school, and hard at work. Dixie was so much improved in mind and body that she took up her work with zest. Nor was Drury a laggard. He immediately began to lead his class, and his professors frequently exchanged prophecies about his future.

Dixie was troubled, however, by the frequent letters from Marvin Harris. There seemed to be no way of making him understand that his suit was hopeless. His letters were sometimes suppliant, again they were full of jealous chiding while, at other times, they breathed subtle threats and dark hints of what would happen if she married the son of the drunken John Patterson. She had clipped the article she had read on the train, and, once or twice, she had re-read it after receiving such a letter from Marvin. Then, the conversation with her father would recur to her memory and she would put the question aside.

Drury's letters were not frequent, but they were long and cheerful. They were like a tonic to her, and she was continually refreshed and inspired by his noble sentiments. He never referred to Marvin as a rival, nor did he ever twit her about having other admirers. The contrast between his letters and Marvin's was so great that the latter would have been furious had he known the effect on Dixie.

CHAPTER VIII.

LITTLE JIM.

Mr. and Mrs. Miller had urged Jessie to come home to them for many reasons; but she preferred to remain in her new home at Sharman, that she might have the presence and encouragement of Maury. Mrs. Miller went to her in November, and was gratified to find her in such superb health and good spirits. There were few white people at Sharman. It was a "cattleman's town," and most of the residents were Mexicans and cowboys. A few of the citizens, however, were desirable neighbors, and these had very naturally been drawn to each other. Maury and Jessie were already popular with everybody; the Mexican women vied with each other in offers of service and little attentions to Jessie, and the men called Maury "Patrone," a title of honor.

The eventful day drew on apace, and Jessie began to show great fortitude and courage. She approached the Vale of Suffering with a quiet confidence that made her appear to her husband more of a queen than ever. He was anxious and uneasy. More than once, he wished for dear old Dr. McConnell, and was on the point of wiring him, when Mrs. Miller told him it would be altogether impractical. She did not tell him, however, that she was as anxious as he for the event to become history, for she had little faith in what medical assistance was within call.

Bravely, and with confident and joyous anticipation, Jessie entered the dark Vale on Wednesday, and, for three terrible days, she was in the very jaws of Death. None of the watchers expected her to return after the second day. Maury wired for Dr. McConnell; but, unfortunately, that very day, the physician had been called to see Allie, who was again stricken. A strong body and a determined will conquered, though, and Jessie came back from the somber shadows on Saturday, and brought with her a young life that she considered fully worth the terrible price she had paid. Her compensation was increased as she saw the new tenderness in her big husband. He was almost afraid to touch the child for fear he would injure it. He would sit speechless in the presence of this great mystery of motherhood. It was a revelation to him of the meaning of Holy Matrimony. His whole being revolted at the remembrance of his early ideas of womankind, and the low standards of life he had made his own. When Mrs. Miller put the week-old baby in his arms, he looked into the dimpled face and wondered what his boy would be like when he was old enough to run about and talk. The tears came to his eyes as he devoutly wished for this mite of humanity a clean, happy, healthy, life. He put the baby on the pillow by its mother as he said:

"Let us call him 'Jim,' Sweetheart. And I hope he will be such a man as his Grandfather Miller."

"Oh Maury! I am so glad you suggested it. That is what I wanted to call him. 'Little Jim Miller Tallman.'"

"Darling, you do not know how I suffered with you. Those terrible days have made me a different man. I have always loved you; now, I cherish you as my own life. I am so glad you survived it all, and I crave the privilege of making your life happy every day you live."

"God has been good to me in giving me such a dear, dear husband. I love you with all my heart."

"Mother," said Jessie, one morning, when the baby was three weeks old, "what can be the matter with Little Jim's eyes? They are swollen and inflamed."

"It is the bright light, I think. He must be kept in the dark for a few days, and he will get all right."

Jessie called the Doctor's attention to it, and he gave her a "wash" for them. Still they grew worse every day until, at last, both eyes were entirely closed by the swelling. The Doctor assured them they would become normal in a few days; but a month went by and they were no better. Jessie regained her strength very slowly, and was able to be up only a part of the time. She was so alarmed that she insisted that they take the little fellow to a specialist. Maury and Mrs. Miller approved of the plan, and, on the day he was two months old, Little Jim was carried into the office of the celebrated Dr. Roberts. The examination had not gone far when a significant glance passed between the Doctor and the office nurse. A treatment was given and they were told to bring the child back the next day. Then began a long course of close treatment for more than a month. Finally, the Doctor invited Maury to dine with him, and, after the meal, took him into the library and said very gently:

"Mr. Tallman, I have very sad news for you. I have done my best to save your baby's eyes, but I have failed. If I could have seen him sooner, I am sure I should have been successful. You might take him to New York, and let Dr. Shaw try his skill. However, I am sure the eyes are gone beyond all possibility of recovery."

Maury Tallman was crushed at the news. He sat in a daze for several minutes; then, he said, in a voice that was scarcely above a whisper:

"Doctor, did I hear aright? Is it possible that my child is really blind? O my God! It cannot be. How can I ever tell his mother? Oh, I would rather die than have Little Jim be blind! I was a fool to allow that old quack to treat him. Why did I not come here at once when his eyes first began to be sore!"

He covered his face with his hands, and his grief was pathetic to behold. Doctor Roberts had broken the same news to other fathers; but this was the most touching incident he had experienced in years.

"Come, Mr. Tallman, don't take it like that. You have done the best you could under the circumstances. He is an extraordinary child, and many blind children are among our best musicians and students. Think of Helen Keller."

"If you will give me a note to Dr. Shaw, I will

take the child to New York, and see what his opinion is."

"Gladly. I will write him the history of the case as far as my connection with it is concerned, and I will be glad to know that you have turned the last stone to recover the sight of the child."

Jessie was scarcely able to undertake the trip; but the excitement made her forget herself, and, the next day, they started for New York. During the trip, Maury broke the news, by degrees, to Jessie. He was afraid she would go down under the blow; but he little knew that women stand such things with more grace and fortitude than men. They are born to trouble, and bear without a murmur pain, suffering, and sorrow that would kill a man.

"What did Doctor Roberts say was the cause of the————?" Jessie could not bring herself to speak the word just yet.

"Ophthalmia, I think he called it."

Even as Maury spoke the word, it was meaningless and almost unheard; for the mother-mind was traveling on through the years, as she would teach the little fingers to feel, and try to tell her first-born of the beauties of Nature and the works of man. From the first moment that she fully understood the meaning of Dr. Robert's report, she knew there was no hope. She did not try to make her husband know how she felt about it; she was simply resigned to what she realized was a certainty.

They both shrank from the other passengers, who were naturally curious about the baby with the bandaged eyes. This was too sacred to share with strangers. This very shrinking from others drove the two sad hearts closer to each other. In after years, Jessie remembered this trip, and all the tender thingsMaury said to her, as well as the pitiful look on his face as he held Little Jim to relieve her. Others might misunderstand him, but she knew him after that; and, through the gloom of her sorrow, these three days with their baby and their grief on the cars shone with a soft light that mellowed her heart and made life bearable.

At Birmingham, they received a message that Allie was worse and another operation would be performed the next week. It must have been that their sorrow over the blindness of the baby had exhausted their grief and rendered them senseless to further shock, for they took the matter very calmly.

On their arrival at New York, they made an engagement with the great specialist, Dr. Shaw. They found him as gentle as a woman, and he impressed them at once that he deserved his reputation for skill. After the second examination, he told them there was no hope of recovering the sight of the child, and he deplored the lack of knowledge and skill that had allowed the disease to pass the stage of possible cure.

The Doctor's final decision dazed Maury, and he went about as one in a trance; but Jessie faced the inevitable with courage and resignation. She saw that her husband needed her, and that he must be cheered and helped just now, or the consequences might be fearful. With feminine heroism, she smiled and talked of the teachers they would employ, and of the things she would teach Little Jim to do.

"Just think how much worse it might be, dear," she said to him, as they were on their way to Allie's bedside. He might have been deformed, or he might have died. I thank God for allowing us to have him, even blind. And it is not as though he had ever known sight. Only as we tell him will he know what he lacks."

"I know, darling; but it is hard for me to take a blind child to your father. He is such a stickler for perfection, even in his stock, that I wanted to show him a perfect child."

"Oh, surely you do not think my father will be that heartless, do you! Why, you will find him the most sympathetic and dearest friend Little Jim will have."

"I am sure of all that. He will pity him; but it is not pity I wanted. I had the fond hope that we would present to your parents one of the finest and most perfect grandchildren that ever came into the world. My disappointment in that regard is almost as keen as my grief over the affliction of the baby."

"Isn't there a modicum of selfish pride in that!"

"Yes, there is. But is it not a pardonable pride!"

"No, I am afraid it is wrong. We have done our best, and I have nothing to chide myself for, nor have you."

"I do chide myself for delaying so long about getting him to competent hands. I wish I had never heard of Sharman. If we had had a real doctor there, our baby would be smiling at us, instead of lying there with his little eyes all bandaged. I tell you it is more than I can bear."

"Come, now, Maury, you must not give way like this. My husband is a strong man, and he can rise above all this and help me to make the best of things as they are."

"Forgive me, dear. I will help you. Let me nurse him a while." He took the mite in his arms, and they changed the conversation.

A surprise awaited them at the station where Allie lived. Maxwell was there in his automobile, and Mr. and Mrs. Miller, accompanied by Jack and Dixie, were waiting for them. Jessie comprehended the meaning of it all in a moment: Allie was desperately ill!

They could not bring themselves to tell the result of their visit to the specialist until they arrived at the house. Dixie held the baby and kept asking how his eyes were until Jessie succeeded in signaling to her to be quiet. Mrs. Miller had prepared Jim by telling him her doubts that the child would ever see again. The others, however, knew nothing more than that the little eyes were affected in some way.

In the presence of duty, Maury's strength returned, and he took Mr. Miller aside when they arrived at the house and told him all that had happened saying that he had hoped to bring to him a perfect child, but had been denied that great pleasure.

Mr. Miller's face showed plainly the agony he felt as he grasped Tallman's hand and said: "You have done your best, my son, and I see you are unjust to yourself in the matter. If you were to blame you might have cause to feel as you do; but, when all this is the result of a combination of circumstances over which you had no control, I want you to know that you have my sympathy and approval. Let us make the best of things as they are, and not think of what might have been."

"Your words comfort me, Mr. Miller. I have suffered all kinds of torment during the past two weeks. It will be an abiding sorrow in my life; but I shall try not to allow it to reflect itself in the lives of my loved ones."

Dixie and Jack were awestricken by the calamity. Mrs. Miller had believed from the first that the affection was fatal to Little Jim's sight, while Allie was suffering too acutely to give expression to her thoughts more than to pull Jessie's head down to her pillow and whisper her love and regrets. The Wrights were as kind and sympathetic as they could possibly be, and interest was soon centered in Allie, and the operation that was to take place two days later.

CHAPTER IX.

ALLIE'S RELEASE.

The deepest snow that had fallen in twenty years lay like a winding sheet over the landscape, and the bare trees scarcelv obstructed the view from the upper windows of Maxwell Wright's residence. Dixie Miller had never seen more than a light fall of snow, which had melted within an hour or two after it fell. She was awakened by the jingling of sleigh-bells Tuesday morning, and, peeping from her window, she was entranced by the world of whiteness. The ground had been bare the night before, and the sky overcast with gray clouds; this morning, the sky was clear, and the air crisp and cold. The sun was just rising, like a ball of fire, and the snow-crystals were gleaming like star-dust.

Already the sleighs were breaking the roads, boys and men with shovels were clearing the walks, and the desire to get out and feel the tingle made Dixie dress hurriedly. She called Jack, and, very soon, the two were on the lawn, frolicking like young animals. All the snow they had ever seen had been wet; but this was light and dry. It flew everywhere, and one could not make a hard ball of it. They found great sport in shaking showers of it from the shrubbery and trees, and in rolling in the deep banks of it along the walks. Dixie remarked that it almost took the place of her plunge in the pool at Tamalpias, while Jack declared that it was more sport than riding the waves at Galveston.

Jessie was awakened by their shouts of glee, and aroused Maury. Neither of them had seen a heavy snow before, and they gazed like children at the white wonder.

"Let's show Little Jim!" cried Jessie. Then she remembered and, together, they turned from the glorious sight to the sleeping babe.

Below in the great old-fashioned four-poster, Allie lay. This was the day appointed for the operation. She had rested well through the night, and, now, she was watching Jack and Dixie playing in the snow near her window. It was a sight so inspiring that the nurse propped her up that she might take in the whole scene. Presently, Maxwell came into the room and greeted her.

"Look, dear, isn't it beautiful! O the pure, white snow. I never saw so much of it before."

"Yes, little woman, it is beautiful, and pure, and white, but not more so than my darling wife. I as so glad you have rested well through the night, and that you are so much better prepared to stand the ordeal of today than we had hoped you would be. How I wish I could take your place and bear it all for you."

"I am glad you can't. You have a great future before you. The world needs you; it can get along without me better than many another."

"I do wish you would be more hopeful, Allie,

I am sure you will get along all right. Why, you will be well again in a few months, and we wil go to Canada again in the summer."

A smile flitted over her face. "That summer was worth all. Weren't we happy!"

"Yes it was a paradise without a serpent in it."

"Indeed it was!"

Then, after a pause: "Do you remember my dream, Maxwell?"

"Yes, I remember. Why?"

"I fear I will not awaken this time before the white horse carries me away," she said very calmly the while stroking his hair with a pale hand.

"Darling, I can't give you up now. You must stay with me a while longer. Please take courage and determine that you will live and get well again." He was restraining himself to the limit of his will-power for her sake. She would need all her strength if she came back from the Valley.

Slowly she shook her head and looked over the snow-covered estate.

"I do not fear to go. There is only one thing that I would care to live for—my dear boy's sake. Nothing else matters. I know you will be always true and good; and I have your promise to be of service to the world. You have begun to live on a higher plane these last few months, and I am sure you will so live that we shall meet again where there will be 'no more curse,' and God will wipe all tears from our eyes. Tell me, dear boy, that, no matter what comes, you will take care of yourself and make the very best of life."

"O Allie, my wife, my idol. I will. Whether you live or die, I shall be a better man than I ever would have been, had I not met you. But I just can not give up hope that you will get well."

"God knows I would not talk to you this way, my dear Maxwell, if I did not feel sure that it is our last sweet conference together. The Doctor has set ten o'clock as the hour, because he wants me to have the advantage of the morning freshness. Kiss me now, dear, then come to me a few moments, after breakfast. I shall want to see each of my loved ones a moment. Tell Dr. McConnell to come in and be with me while I talk to them."

The nurse insisted that she must rest, and Maxwell swallowed his sobs and left the room. He went immediately to his own room, however, and there gave way to the torrent of grief that he had kept pent up in his breast while he had talked with the invalid. When he did not appear at breakfast, Maury went to his room to look for him, and there the two men comforted each other. It was hard to tell whose sorrow was the keenest, that of the husband who was facing the grim reaper who was ready to snatch away the wife of his bosom, or that of the father whose baby son was doomed to a life of darkness. It is here set down to the credit of both that each found a balm for his wound in trying to comfort the other.

The gloom deepened and spread, until it encompassed the whole household. Even young, vigorous Jack was overcome by it. Jessie found herself weak and almost sick from her long trip, and Dixie was of such a sympathetic nature that she remarked to her mother that it seemed strange God would make everything so dazzlingly white outside, when there was so much sadness and gloom within. Mrs. Miller was everywhere, cheering this one and encouraging that one, waiting on Jessie, nursing the baby, counseling Maxwell, and keeping Jim from being lonesome and sad.

It was evident that Dr. McConnell was not at all optimistic about the result of the operation. He even dropped a few hints that were intended to prepare the family for the worst. He was in the sick-room at nine o'clock, when the family came in to see Allie, and he shrewdly managed to keep them all in good cheer, and led the conversation away from the serious. It took all his tact to accomplish this end, for the patient wanted to talk to them as she had to her husband. At last, she kissed each, and told them good-by in a manner that left nothing to be said in reply, and the Doctor and the nurse got them out of the room as quickly as possible. Maxwell had a few minutes with her, then went to his room to suffer the untold agonies of suspense and uncertainty until the ordeal should be over.

Dr. Duncan and his assistants arrived promptly

at ten. It was unusual for him to agree to operate outside of the hospital; but he made an exception in this case because the hospital was crowded, and it would be easy to make the room in the home sanitary. Indeed, it was already so under his careful instructions.

Again, one of the Miller twins entered the Valley of Shadows and took the leading part on the stage of tragedy. The dark, shrouded form of Death, peered with hungry, lustful eyes over the shoulders of the surgeons, while white-winged angels hovered near to cheat the monster of his victim even if he should gain the victory. It was a tense hour, and pulses quickened and slowed as the pendulum of life swung back and forth. Dr. McConnell, holding the pulse of the woman at whose birth he had attended, scarcely breathed as he watched the progress of the battle. Twice, he was compelled to ask the great surgeon to wait until the pulse of the patient recovered somewhat.

At last, it was finished, and only the closing of the wound remained to be accomplished. Dr. Duncan shook his head and said:

"It is just as well, if she had recovered, she would have been a hopeless, suffering invalid, and, very likely, she would have been insane. Very few escape insanity after an operation like this."

Dr. McConnell dropped the wrist he was holding and turned away, sobbing like a schoolboy. He loved Jim Miller's children, even as they loved him. It is a sad day that sees the passing of these dear old family doctors. They did not know as much medical science as the physicians of today; but they knew human hearts better, and their kindly smiles and tender touch was worth more than their medicine in many cases. Their knowledge of the family, and its history and predispositions, gave them a wonderful advantage. Among the heroes of America, let us never forget the Old Family Doctor.

At eleven o'clock, the doctors left the room, but the reaper, Death, remained, and the angels hovered closer over the quiet form of Allie. The family came, and the husband. They knew, now, why her last word had been "good-by." Mr. and Mrs. Wright had come, and Maxwell needed them. His quiet grief was pitiful to behold. For two hours, they watched as black pinions and white drew closer and closer. At times, they thought both had departed, but the beloved one was going to sleep very quietly. No one saw them, and none heard the rustle of their wings; however, they were there, and, soon after noon, the band of angels snatched up the Lily Death had cut down, and bore it out and away from the snow-clad earth, beyond the shining sun, and out to the City not made with hands.

When she was gone, her old "black mammy," who had been lurking near the door, came and knelt beside the bed in uncontrollable grief.

"O God," she cried, "didn't I say dem clouds You done gib 'em dat weddin'-day meant nothin' but sorrer and def? He'er's my po' baby-twin done gone home to Glory, and he'er's Little Jim all blin', and neber will see no mo'. O God, I wants ter die, too. Marse Jim, luk at dat sweet angel-chile. Ain't she dat purty, jes' lak a lily-bud? Ole Missus, I sho' lubs yo' all, an' I wishes ter God I could b'ar it all fer you. Come he'er, Miss Jessie you po' dahlin' chile and let me see yo' all together once mo' fo' I dies."

Thus with family, husband, black mammy, and family physician about her, Allie Miller was released from the curse that lies on womankind. The tragedy had been enacted and hungry, lustful Death had glutted himself on his victim. But only for a while; for, at the resurrection of the just, he will have to give up the body, even as he was cheated of the soul of his victim, and all through the Child of a woman. Ah, then we will cry in derision: "O Grave, where is thy victory, Death, where is thy sting!"

They carried the body back to the Sunny South and laid it by the grandparents in the beautiful cemetery at Tamalpias. The transition from the frozen North to the lilacs and hyacinths of the South seemed like a symbol of her going from this cold, cruel world to the plains of Paradise. The whole town went to the cemetery, even to the negroes for miles around. Maxwell Wright was given a glimpse of Southern sympathy and hospitality that he had never dreamed existed; and his parents, who had come with him, saw things far different from what they had expected. Indeed, these are the incidents that teach us most effectively that we are one people, and that our joys and sorrows are the same, and our interests are identical, North and South.

The Wrights remained with the Millers for two months, and Maury and Jessie took up their burden and their blind child and went back to the little town near the Rio Grande. Dixie returned to school, and old Rilla went about the place forlorn and uncomforted.

Drury Patterson wrote to both Dixie and her father, and offered condolence and sympathy. Marvin Harris wrote to Dixie also; but he used it more as an occasion for pressing his suit for her hand than for trying to heal the wound in her heart. He did not tell her that he was paying attention to Thelma Dawson; however, she had heard of it during the few days she was at home. Nor did she care; she was glad that he was attracted to some one else. It only disgusted her that he should write to her like that when she was sure he was saying the same things to Thelma.

The Wrights left for home on May-day, when the fields were green and the flowers blooming in luxury everywhere. The symbol had changed for Maxwell Wright, now. He felt that his life from now on would be like the bare trees of New York State, which had been retarded by a very late spring. If he had gone away sorrowing, he came back sad, but not as sad as he would be when his eyes were opened to the secret of the Great Tragedy, and he was destined to be initiated into that secret in the near future. There is no curse without a just cause, and the cause lies nearer mankind than it does to the Creator. Remove the cause and the curse will vanish.

CHAPTER X.

A STARTLING REVELATION.

Mrs. Miller dropped the magazine she was reading, and looked at her husband with such a pall of terror showing in her face, that he started from his chair and made quick inquiry.

"What is the matter, Mollie? Are you ill? You are as pale as a corpse."

"Jack, please leave the room; I want to speak to your father."

Jack left the room, and Mrs. Miller turned to reply to her husband's question.

"No, I am not ill. James, do you believe it is possible that, if a young man sows wild oats, his wife and children will have to bear the consequences?"

"In what way? What do you mean?"

"Well, here is an article by Miss Helen Keller, the remarkable blind woman, in which she declares that social sin is the most common cause of blindness, and that ——"

It was not like Jim Miller to be rude: but he strode across the room and snatched the magazine from her lap, saying:

"Where is it? Show it to me."

"Here, the first thing in the magazine."

She watched him as he read it, watched his face grow red, then white, and finally ashen. Then, as he finished, she heard his teeth click, and saw his lips compress, as he rose and started to leave the room with the journal in his hand.

"Where are going, James?'" she asked.

"I am going to interview Dr. McConnell. I'll be back in a short time; don't worry, dear."

It took him only a moment to crank the big red machine, which he had recently purchased, and, ten minutes later, he was standing in the Doctor's office, exclaiming:

"Dr. McConnell, I want you to tell me the truth, and the whole truth. Is it possible that the suffering and death of my child, the affliction of my grandchild, and the invalidism of my daughter, Jessie, is due to the dissolute habits of the men who married my twins?"

"My dear Mr. Miller, you are plainly excited. Pray sit down and tell me what you mean."

"This is what I mean. Here is an article by Helen Keller, the blind young woman, who has gained a college education through her finger-tips. I want to read it to you and ask you some questions."

"Very well, but allow me to say before you begin that most articles of that kind are written by novices, who know very little of the subjects on which they write, and they generally exaggerate the facts and paint them to appeal to the public."

"That may be true, indeed I am sure it is, in most cases; but, if it so in this instance, you will know it. This is a scientific subject, and we may arrive at the facts. It is for that reason I have come to you. You have known me and mine for twenty-five years; I trust you implicitly, and shall expect you to give me the unvarnished truth in this matter."

"I shall do my best for you, Jim. Now, read the article to me."

"In order that you may get the whole matter before you in a comprehensive way. I will read the article, and then we can talk about it. She says:

"Once I believed that blindness, deafness, tuberculosis, and other causes of human suffering, were necessary, unpreventable; I believed that we must accept blind eyes, deaf ears, diseased lungs as we accept the havoc of tornadoes and deluges, and that we must bear with them with as much fortitude as we could gather from religion and philosophy. But gradually my reading extended, and I found that those evils are to be laid, not at the door of Providence, but at the door of mankind; that they are, in a large measure, due to ignorance, stupidity, and sin.

"The most common cause of blindness is ophthalmia of the new-born. One pupil in every three in the Institute for the Blind in New York City was blinded in infancy by this disease; nearly all of the sixteen babes in the Sunshine Home, in Brooklyn; six hundred sightless persons in the State of New York; between six thousand and seven thousand persons in the United States, were plunged into darkness by ophthalmia of the new-born.

"What is the cause of ophthalmia neonatorium? It is a specific germ communicated to the child by the mother at birth. Previous to the child's birth, she has unconsciously received it through infection by her husband. In mercy let it be remembered, the father does not know he has so foully destroyed the eyes of his child and handicapped him for life. It is a part of the bitter harvest of the 'Wild Oats' he has sown. Society has smiled on his 'youthful recklessness,' because Society does not know that 'they enslave their children's children who make compromise with sin.'

"Society has yet to learn that the blind beggar at the street corner, the epileptic child, the woman on the operating table, are the wages of 'youthful indiscretion.' Today, science is verifying what the Old Testament taught three thousand years ago, and the time has come when there is no longer the excuse of ignorance. Knowledge has been given us; it is our part to apply it.

"Of the consequences of social sin, blindness is by no means the most terrible. The same infection that blots out the eyes of the baby is responsible for many childless homes; for thousands of cases of lifelong invalidism; for eighty per cent. of all the inflammatory diseases peculiar to woman; and for seventy-five per cent. of all operations performed on mothers to save their lives."

Jim Miller stopped and sobbed. The tears blinding his eyes and a thousand emotions were struggling within him for supremacy. The old Doctor sat very quiet. His eyes, too, were full of tears, and he was dreading the talk that must follow. But Jim Miller had not finished reading.

"The day has come when women must face the truth. They cannot escape the evil unless they have the knowledge that saves. Must we leave young girls to meet the danger in the dark because we dare not turn the light on our social wickedness? False delicacy and prudery must give place to precise information and common sense. It is high time to abolish falsehood and let the plain truth come in. Out with the cowardice that shuts the eyes to immorality that causes disease and human misery. I am confident that, when the people know the truth, the day of deliverance for mother and child will be at hand.

"We must set to work, in the right direction, the three great agencies which inform and educate us: the Church, the School, and the Press. If they remain silent, obdurate, they must bear the odium that recoils upon evil-doers. They may not listen, at first, to our pleas for light and knowledge. They may combine to baffle us; but there will rise, again and again, to confront them, the beseeching forms of little children — deaf, blind, crooked of limb, and vacant of mind."

The latter part of the article was read brokenly, and there were many pauses to allow the lump that was in the reader's throat to recede. As he finished, the paper fell from his hands, and he sat for some minutes as one dazed. He was uncertain how to begin the questions that he felt were already answered. At last, he laid a hand on the Doctor's knee, and asked:

"Tell me, Doctor, is it all true?"

"I am sorry to have to tell you that you may consider Miss Keller an authority on the subject. She has written wisely and well."

"I am to understand, then, that my child died, after her awful suffering, because she married a man who had sowed wild oats?"

"I was present at both operations, and I can speak advisedly: undoubtedly, Allie's trouble was solely the result of this infection."

"And my child went to the surgeon's table and to her grave, the innocent victim of the 'necessary evil.' O my God! Is it possible!"

Dr. McConnell had never seen a strong man so moved as Jim Miller was that day, as he faced the truth about social sin.

"Don't take it so hard, my friend. It was terrible, I know; but it is only one case out of multiplied thousands. All about you are the victims of this same monster."

Jim looked up, and there was despair in his voice as he asked: "And Little Jim—that is the cause of his blindness?"

"Dr. Roberts says it is ophthalmia."

"And did you know all this before my girls married?"

"Not as I know it now. You see, we are just discovering these things. I knew that many of our troubles arose from the profligate lives of our young men; but I have learned much in that regard within the last two years."

"You must have known whether Maury Tallman was fit to marry my child."

"Do you forget that we talked of that very thing before the twins married, and I told you that I was sure Mr. Wright had sown wild oats. You treated the matter lightly, then."

"That is what is killing me. I prided myself in my stock, and I would not breed even a hog to a defective animal; but I gave my girls away to diseased men. What a fool I have been. Oh, by a thousand times, I would rather my twins had died in infancy than that they should have come to this!"

"But you did not know."

"No, I did not know. And why? Because of the 'ethics' of the medical profession. Every doctor who knows of these things, and then lets his patients go on and marry under such circumstances is a party to the crime. Would you allow your own child to marry such a man?"

"I am glad you ask that question. You will not be so bitter toward me when you know that I have been fighting for six months to keep my daughter, Mrs. Hawkes, off the operating table, and I suspect I have lost the battle. No, I did not exactly know that Bert Hawks was not fit to marry her; but I knew that he had led a fast life. So you see, I, too, have had my awakening, and I can sympathize with you as few men can. I have determined to use my utmost endeavor to protect innocent lives hereafter, no difference what the cost to me."

"You infer that all men who have been 'fast' are physically unfit to marry. Is that true?"

"Yes! Recent investigations disclose the fact

that four out of five young men over eighteen years old have been infected by the germs God has appointed to live in the wild oats patch to punish all who enter there. And, once diseased, they are never fit to marry your daughter or mine."

"Then why, in the name of womanhood, haven't we laws on our statute-books forbidding them to marry?"

"That is coming. I hope to live until the time when all applicants for marriage license will have to get certificates from reputable physicians attesting to their physical fitness to marry."

For some minutes, Jim Miller looked out of the window at the clouds all tinged with the glow of sunset. Then, he turned and spoke with great earnestness.

"Would to God I had known all this three years ago. I feel something akin to murder in my heart toward the men who have ruined my daughters. But I must grip myself and do my best for all concerned. We have laws on our statute-books for the protection of our cattle, horses, hogs, and even for our dogs and wild birds; but, while we have the inspector writing a permit to move cattle that are free of ticks, the minister is marrying our children to persons who have all kinds of diseases. It is a travesty on the name of civilization. I shall offer myself as a candidate for the next legislature, and my platform will be along these lines. Meantime, I want you to promise me that you will give me a report on any young man I may send to you for examination before he can marry Dixie. That man does not live who can get my consent to marry her until I am satisfied on this point. I haven't another daughter to sacrifice on the altar of our social wickedness."

"Jim Miller, you are a real man. I believe God has allowed all this to come to you to arouse you for the defense of future generations. Send your man to me whenever you get ready, and I will exhaust my skill for the protection of your other child. Also I will help you in your fight by giving you all the data and help I can."

"I thank you, Dr. McConnell. I shall rely on your assistance in many ways. I am going to have this article by Miss Keller printed and use it in my campaign; and, if you see other articles along this line, clip them for me. This State is going to have some light on this subject whether I am elected or not."

Jim Miller stood in the gathering gloom of the Doctor's office, and, to the man of medicine, he looked like a Moses in dignity, a Daniel in purpose, and a Lincoln in calm determination to emancipate the millions of women and children that seemed to cry to him out of their bondage to the passions of depraved manhood. Silently, they shook hands, and Jim Miller went down the stairs and got into his automobile. His first intention was to drive home to his wife; but he did not feel ready to tell her what he knew and felt, so he drove the car down the river-road. The full moon was rising over the tree-tops and the evening air felt gracious to his hot brow. Five miles from town, he stopped the car on the bank of the clear stream, and sat listening to the night-sounds about him. Across the river, a whippoor-will was calling to his mate, somewhere a cow was lowing, and all nature was tranquil and beautiful. The lines of the poet came to him with new meaning:

"Only man is vile."

Then, he gazed up at the stars. Somewhere, out there, his child was beyond the reach of it all. He bared his head and sighed deeply. Then, he reached out a hand toward the twinkling stars and cried:

"O Allie, my beautiful child. I shall give my life to save others from the Valley of Shadows. If only I may do that, I shall not have lived in vain. That shall be my revenge, and I will leave all else to God."

Then he turned the car toward home.

Mrs. Miller was waiting for him with great anxiety. She wanted to know the result of his interview, and he had been gone so long that she was frightened.

"I beg you pardon, dear," he said gently. "I was longer than I thought. I could not come back until I had time to think, so I drove down the river, and, see, I am calm now. The storm has passed, and I am a better man."

He told her the whole horrible truth. He knew she was strong enough to bear it, for she was the mother of that other woman who had so nobly borne the shock of her child's blindness. It is uncertainty that kills a woman, and it was a relief to this one to know the things her husband had to tell her. Most of it was a revelation to her; she had been reared far away from the wickedness of the towns and cities, and knew nothing of their vice.

When he had finished, she looked up into his face and said: "James, dear, I am so glad God gave me a pure man for a husband."

"Yes, darling wife, I met you at the altar as pure as I expected you to be. I never went into the wild oats patch; my mother stood between me and that kind of life. I could not go there thinking of her. I thank God she saved me, and thus saved you, and our children. But to think that two of our girls have become victims of men who think their sin a 'necessary evil' makes my blood surge in my veins. That is the thing I have had to conquer today."

"I am so glad you have conquered. We will leave the punishment to One who is wiser than we. Oh, what a cruel world! And to think of the thousands that are suffering what Jessie is suffering, and hordes are going to their graves as Allie went. Can we do nothing to save them?"

"That is another question I have settled this evening. I told Dr. McConnell that I am going to offer for the next legislature, and I shall try to pass some laws for the control of this very matter. I have not had time to think it all out yet, but I am sure there will be a way to regulate the marriage contract so that a girl will be safe in going to the altar with a man. And we will have to plan to educate our young, too. We can only hope to have restrictive laws as an expedient until we can educate the next generation."

"How you cheer my heart, James. I want to help you in this great work. We will just give our lives to it. We have money enough to make an effective campaign, and it will be so much better than giving your time to improving stock."

"Yes, I will give the same attention, and more, to the improvement of men that I have always given to horses and cattle. It is a great undertaking for a man who has never been a platform speaker. I will have to learn politics, and I will have to study this question until I become an authority on it. I shall go to the city tomorrow and provide myself with the best library to be had, and I shall consult the best medical authority in the State. I wish I was twenty years younger."

"You will do better that you are a mature man. I am proud of you tonight, my husband. God bless you, and may you accomplish this great thing for the race."

CHAPTER XI.

DIXIE'S PROMISE.

The next morning Jim Miller left his breakfast untasted, and took a long walk up the creek to Indian Bluff. He had slept little, and he was having a battle yet this morning. Dixie would be home from school during the week, and his concern for her was deep. He had decided that he must warn her of the danger that had taken her sisters unawares; but how to go about it, and just how much to tell her; how to bring the message home to her heart without giving her a shock or embittering her against all mankind, and the problem of her having so fully given Drury Patterson her heart that she would marry him anyway; these were the questions that he pondered as he sat on the Bluff and watched a pair of white cranes catching fish in the creek below.

The Bluff was of soft stone, and every visitor had scratched his or her name on the smooth surface. His eyes caught the names of Jessie and Maury written together, and then Allie's and Maxwell Wright's, with the date, "April 20, 19——." That was the day they had become engaged, and he turned sick at heart as he looked at the inscription. It was as though he was at her grave and this was her tombstone. Then, he saw Dixie's name, and Drury Patterson's under it, and the date was not quite a year in the past. He could stand no more, so he crawled down and walked back across the fields.

His face was so white and drawn when his wife came to the parlor to answer his summons, that she inquired if he was feeling badly.

"Yes, Mollie, I am heart-sick. I have been trying to solve the problem of protecting Dixie from the tragedy that has overtaken her sisters, and I have come to the settled conviction that there is only one way to do it. She must be told the truth about the whole matter, and warned against marrying such a man."

"I agree with you on that. I, too, have been thinking, and I am concerned for both of the children. You must talk to Dixie; you can do that better than I can. I can talk to Jack, and will do so; but I want you to talk to Dixie."

"I have fought all that out; I want to talk to her so she will have confidence in me to protect her, and I want to impress her so deeply that she will not allow her heart to influence her head when the test comes."

"I am going to have Jack read the article by Miss Keller; then, I am going to talk to him. I want him to be as pure as his sister."

"Yes, indeed. I am going to the city today, as I had planned, and I shall come back by Traskwood, and bring Dixie home with me."

It was a week later that Jim Miller sent for his daughter to come to the library. When Dixie entered the room, she found him sitting with his face in his hands. She went to him and put her hand on his head.

"What is it, Daddy?"

"Sit down, Dixie, I want to talk to you. Do you believe your father loves you?"

"Why Daddy, what a question! I know you love me."

"Well, out of the love I bear you, my child, I want to talk very seriously to you this morning. You are almost a mature woman, and I hope you will not be shocked at what I have to say. I would rather, however, be tied to a post and lashed with a horsewhip, than to have to tell you this sad story. I have always been a proud man—too proud—but I am humbled today with the knowledge that my sex is weak and wicked. We talked frankly about alcoholism last year. But that is a simple question compared with this. I have an article here that I want to read to you. Then, we must plan for your protection."

When the reading was done, he told her all; and, noble girl that she was, she saw his suffering and made it easier for him by looking him in the face the while, and speaking a word now and then to put him at his ease. As he finished telling her of his plans and purposes, he took her hand in his and said:

"And now, daughter, I want you to promise me that you will not marry Drury Patterson nor any other man untill he shall bring me a certificate from the physician that I select that he has never been contaminated by these diseases."

She looked at him steadily for a full minute. Then she flung her arms about his neck, and sobbed:

"Daddy, will you protect me like that?"

"Yes, child, with every drop of blood in my veins."

"You are the best daddy in the world. Of course, I will promise you. I do promise. How I do love you, and how I admire your courage in talking to me about it, when I could tell you were suffering in the effort."

"Suffer! Oh, how I have suffered since I found all this out, only last week! I had a battle about telling you, partly because of my proud disposition, and partly because it is a delicate subject for a father to talk to his grown daughter about."

"But is it not a father's place to talk to his daughter when there is so much at stake?"

"That is true. Yet it does not make the task any the less delicate. Thank God, it is done, and I want you to have all confidence in me. Whenever you want me to, I will investigate the man who wants to marry you. I shall not try to prevent your marrying; for there are pure, good men, and I shall be glad to receive any man as a son-in-law, if you love him, and he is worthy to be your husband."

"What do you think of Drury?"

"I am pretty well satisfied that he is a gentleman in every sense of the word. But we can not afford to make any mistakes, and he will have to undergo the same tests that any other man would."

"Of course; but I am sure he is clean."

"That is my only fear about the future. Surely 'love covers a multitude of sins,' and most women will marry the man they love even if they know they are to suffer by it."

"But I will not. I will never marry any man unless he can come to me as pure as I go to him."

"I am glad to hear you say it. I had rather you would die today, than that you live to suffer as Allie did, or that you should be the mother of a child like Little Jim."

"Does mother know all this?"

"Yes; she and I talked it all over, and she asked me to talk to you. Go and tell her to come here."

When she came, Dixie repeated her promise to them both. Mrs. Miller slipped her arm about the girl's waist and drew her to her heart.

"My child, you have the best father in the world."

"That's what I told him. And I have the sweetest mother in the world, too. Haven't I, Daddy?"

"Yes, indeed!"

The two old lovers kissed each other; then, they kissed the daughter whom they were undertaking to protect. It was a great day in the Miller household. Jim Miller performed another hard task that day. He wrote to Maxwell Wright. Kindly, yet plainly, he told him what he had discovered, and asked him to read the article Miss Keller had written; and he advised him that he must never marry another woman, lest he bring her down as Allie had gone. His hardest task was to keep back the reproach he felt; but he succeeded wonderfully. The intimate acquaintance with the Wright family gave him more charity than he would have had otherwise.

He made two or three attempts to write to Maury Tallman; but, each time, he tore the letter up, and ended by deciding to wait until he could talk to him face to face. Who knows whether he made a mistake or not? It will take eternity to reveal.

Although Dixie was sure of Drury's innocence, she found herself under a peculiar restraint when in his presence. He noticed it and twitted her pleasantly about it; but she could not overcome it. She studied his parents more closely than she had ever done before. She visited Mrs. Patterson in her home, and she was delighted to find her a cultured woman. She was crushed by the dissipation of her husband, and by their financial straits; but she impressed Dixie as a fine character who had been limited by her environment.

Drury was making fine progress in his study of medicine, and, during this summer, he was working at the Palace Drug Store. He had had his eyes opened to a great deal by hearing the lectures at the University, and his astonishment was great when he found how wicked young men of the little village of Tamalpias were. Dr. McConnell took much interest in him, and told him much. He even secured the article Jim Miller had read to him, and had the young man read it. Hiis delight was great when Drury expressed himself very clearly on the subject, and told him how glad he was that he had never sowed wild oats. Encouraged by this, the Doctor told him of his interview with Jim Miller, and of that man's plans for the salvation of the race, also of his decision that only a clean man could have his daughter.

"I certainly am thankful you have told me all this, Doctor. Perhaps you know I have been corresponding with Miss Dixie?"

"No," exclaimed the Doctor, in some surprise, "I did not know that, or perhaps I should not have spoken so frankly."

"I am glad you did speak freely to me. I love Dixie Miller, and I thank God I am worthy, physically, to marry her when I get through school and am settled. If I was not clean, I would never marry. I am in favor of Mr. Miller's proposed laws, and am sure he will have no opposition except from those who could not get the certificates. I shall keep myself pure, never doubt that."

"I have always liked you, Drury, and I want you to finish school and come into this office with me. I am getting old and shall have to retire within a few years, and I want you to succeed me in my large practice."

"You embarrass me, Doctor. I appreciate your most kind offer, and, if I should decide to settle down to a general practice, nothing would suit me better. But I am seriously inclined to surgery. If I should become a surgeon, I want to be the very best, and would likely have to locate in a city."

Dr. McConnell looked at the boy for several seconds before replying. His own son had disappointed him; for he had wanted Tom to be a surgeon, but Tom had frittered away his school-days with athletics, and now was a worn-out baseball player. If only Tom had been such a young man as this child of drunken John Patterson! Then, he spoke to Drury again.

"There is only one lion in your path, son, and that is the beast that slew your father's manhood and will-power. You may not know it, but it is a fact that a child inherits his father's appetites and passions, as well as his predispositions to disease. Have you ever desired to drink any kind of stimulants?"

"Never in my life. The very smell of whiskey is repulsive to me."

"Splendid! You must be careful, though. A doctor's life is so strenuous, and he is called at all hours of the night, until, after a while, he feels that a little stumulant or a drug will brace him up and help him to be more alert and efficient. He takes an occasional drink, or dose, and it is not long before he is a slave to the habit. If you ever start like that, you will awaken all that you have inherited from your father, and your course will be swift and brief."

Drury reddened at the straightforward words, and he realized, as never before, what it meant to be a child of a drunkard.

"Isn't it strange, Doctor, that I haven't this appetite, if I am ever to have it?"

"Yes! You are now past twenty-one years old

and one would expect that there would be some indication of the tendency. Really, it is remarkable that you are so clear of it. I do not know that I have ever known a case where the only child of such a father was entirely averse to the taste and smell of whiskey. It is passing strange; and, if you will pardon me for saying it, I don't see any of John Patterson's habits or looks about you. You are as different as a child can be from his parent. Nor do you resemble your mother. I never saw her people; but you must get your looks and predispositions from them."

"I have wondered at all this myself. Mother has never told me a thing about her people. I do not know where they live. She seems to prefer that I never know about them. I know all the Pattersons, and I have never seen one that I look at all like, nor do I seem to have anything in common with them."

"Well, let us hope that you will not develop any of the Patterson traits. They are all good people in their way, but they are all dissipated. Remember that I am your friend, and come to me with any of your problems. I will help you in any way that I can."

Drury always made friends like that. He did not try to win them; they came to him naturally; and, once a friend to him, they were always for him. He never lost a friend.

CHAPTER XII.

THE PRICE MAURY PAID.

When Maxwell Wright received Jim Miller's letter, he hurried out to a news-stand and purchased the magazine Mr. Miller had referred to, and immediately read the article. The effect on him was not so rapid as it had been on his father-in-law; it required more time for the whole thing to become comprehensive. That is the difference between the Northern man and the Southern. Your Southerner is quick, impulsive, rash; he thinks of murder and revenge more readily than the citizen of the North. The Northern man puts more value on life, and the Southern man puts more on virtue. If one violates social law at the North, he or she is ostracized; but, if a Southern home is invaded, there is murder, and the defense pleads the unwritten law.

So Maxwell Wright sat down to digest the matter. At first, he was inclined to scoff at the very idea. What did a woman—and a woman that had been blind all her life—know about such thing, anyway? Why, he knew many young men that had gone the same gaits he had, and their wives were neither invalids nor their children blind. Well, there was Wilbur Thomas; his wife was operated on, and both his children deformed. Yes, and Sam Yoe's wife died within a year after their marriage. But some persons are going to die anyway, and women have always had trouble.

Then, he read the letter and the article again. This time, the matter took a more serious aspect in his mind. He determined to have a talk with Dr. Duncan. But the Doctor was out of the city and would not return for a week. He did not have a friend he could talk to, so he decided to write to Maury Tallman. Jim Miller had mentioned the fact of the baby's blindness, and Maxwell felt that he and Maury were fellow sufferers; if he could not write to him, whom could he consult with? Very likely, Mr. Miller had written him, too, and he wondered how the fine fellow had taken it.

Afterward, he wished he had not written. But who could have foreseen the crisis impending?

Maury Tallman was becoming somewhat reconciled to the blindness of Little Jim when he received the letter from New York. Business was good, and he was in better spirits than he had been for years. The bookkeeper brought in the mail, and he had gone through most of it when he came on Maxwell's letter. They had not written many letters to each other, and this long, double-postage letter amused him as he opened it.

"Ho, ho," he laughed, "Maxwell has turned missionary and is sending me a bundle of tracts. Well, I guess I need them in this heathenish place."

Then, he began to read.

"What on earth does he mean? 'It seems we are both under the same condemnation. If the blind woman is right, I am no less than a murderer, and you have put out the eyes of your own child.' I wonder if he has gone insane over Allie's death, poor fellow. 'I don't believe a word of it, yet. At any rate, I am going to ask Dr. Duncan about it when he comes home next week. Read the article and write me what you think.'"

By the time the letter was finished, it began to dawn on the reader that, in some way, he had caused the loss of his child's eyes, and that, by the same rule, Maxwell was charged with Allie's death.

Then, he took up the clipping and read the words that had caused such a commotion in the Miller home. The effect was altogether different on him from what it had been on Maxwell. The paper rattled in his hands, and the cold perspiration stood on his face. He even groaned so audibly that the bookkeeper asked him if he had received bad news; but he was lost to everything except the words that were being burned into his brain, and they carried the weight of conviction with them. He took them at their full worth, nor questioned their truth for a moment. Before he was half done reading, the letters ran together, and his head fell on the desk before him.

"What is it, Mr. Tallman? I hope you haven't received bad news," and the bookkeeper came near him.

"Yes, quite a shock, Mertens. Bring me a glass of water, please."

When he had taken the water, and had recovered to some extent, he finished reading the paper. Then, he excused himself, saying that he must go home for a little while. He started for the beautiful cottage on the white hill above the business section of the town; but he was too dazed to face his wife just yet; he must have time to get his equilibrium, so he turned out the street that led to a deep, dry canyon, where cactus and yucca relieved the white alkali that made the country so glaring. Arrived at the wall of the canyon, he sat down and went over his past history in detail, dwelling with bitterness on the few incidents that haunted him like specters, and mocked him for having thought there was real pleasure in sin. What he had called "having a little fun," now looked like crime; having "a high old time" had proved to be a revel with Death. Oh, if he could only recall the years of his folly! He had never been reckless and dissipated; only two or three times, while in school, had he been intoxicated; he had been called a "goody-goody" boy by his classmates because he would not take in the town with them; but he had limited his wildness to festal occasions. He had laughed at the penalty assessed against him on one of his "flings," and had considered himself fortunate in being quickly pronounced "all right" by a second-rate doctor, who "practised" for the college boys.

All this, and more, came back to him as he sat there on the brink of the canyon, and he wished he had died before he ever went to college. Then, a dusky face, the f[illegible] of [illegible] s[illegible]ervan[illegible], [illegible]peere at him out of the dim past. That awful curse of the South—two races living practically together—has ruined many young lives. The obsequious, improvident mulatto, with inordinate desires for the finery of her white mistress, and without character or virtue, is a real menace to the adolescent youth. Old Rilla's mutterings had been full of meaning, after all. Oh, how he hated himself!

He broke a leaf off a Spanish Dagger that grew within his reach. Pressing his finger against its needlelike point caused a sharp pain, and he saw a tiny drop of blood where the point had entered. As in a trance, he lifted the leaf and his face was contorted in desperation as the wild desire to prick his eyeballs, and live a life of darkness in sympathy and companionship with his child, entered his tortured mind. This desire grew apace, and would doubtless have mastered him had he not thought of the brand it would put on him. It would be the mark of Cain, and, everywhere he went the story of his guilty crime and criminal guilt would be rehearsed. He thought, also, of the handicap it would put on him in providing for them. The battle raged for more than an hour, and the tortures of the damned can be no keener than those of this lone man, whose refinement and culture only increased his capacity for suffering. One wild idea of self-punishment after another clamored in his brain. If only he had a pistol, he would end it [illegible] moment. Looking [illegible], he could [illegible] just where [illegible] body would fall, and then it would tumble to the next ledge, and, finally, it would land a hundred feet below. He would be missed, and they might search for him; but the vultures, flying high above him, would find the body and pluck out the eyes before the searchers found it and drove them away. Yes, that would be adequate punishment and retribution.

He leaped to his feet with settled determination to get a pistol and commit the deed at once. He argued that he had lost self-respect, and that he could never again face the little woman he had ruined, nor see the child he had deprived of sight. He was unworthy to defile the pure air with his breath, and the sooner he launched out into the unknown, the better it would be for all concerned. He formulated the lie he would tell the dealer as an excuse for wanting the gun, and was almost in the door of the shop when he thought of writing Jessie a letter. He must do that, and write one to Jim Miller, too.

He returned to the bank, and was soon at work writing Jessie. It was hard to begin just right, and he tore up three or four attempts before he got the first paragraph to suit him. Then, it occurred to him that he must give her evidence of the guilt he felt, that would show her how utterly impossible it was for him ever to see the baby's blind eyes again. Would she consider the clipping as conclusive as he knew it must be? The doubt, once suggested, grew graver and graver, until he sat back in his chair and gazed out of the window in perplexed study. Could there be any possible chance that Miss

Keller was wrong? There was only one person in the world who could satisfy his mind on that question, and that person was Dr. Roberts. Like a drowning man, he grasped the straw, and, in another minute, he was at the telephone.

"Hello, dear," he called, "I have a sudden call to go East, and must start on the next train. It leaves within thirty minutes. Could you run down and bring me a hand-bag and some laundry? No, don't try to bring the baby; you will not have time for that. Get Pablo to hitch up, and he can drive you to the station; I'll meet you there. All right. Hurry, now."

He was glad the train was on time, for he wanted to get away. He gave hurried instructions to the assistant cashier, who had come in, and was at the station when Jessie arrived.

"What is the matter, Maury, that you have to hurry off like this? You look troubled. Is there anything wrong?"

"O, it is only a business affair. I have to go to Stockton to look after some matters. Don't worry, dear. If everything is all right, I shall return on the first train. If I am detained, I shall write you to-morrow. Be a good girl, and take care of yourself."

With feminine intuition, she knew something was wrong, and she wished she had time to make him tell her all that was troubling him. But there was only a minute more, the train was even now whistling for the station, and there were people about them.

"Darling," she whispered, "what is it that is troubling you? Tell me."

"I can't now. The train is coming; but it will be all right."

"Is everything all right at the bank?"

"Yes, indeed. Run along now. I shall either be at home to-morrow or you will have a letter from me telling you all about it. If I write, I shall put a special delivery stamp on the letter, so you will get it at once."

He kissed her warmly, and she clung to him until he had to run to catch the step of the train as it pulled out. Her heart ached for the man who was plainly undergoing a crisis in his life. She was scarcely able to be out of bed. Her health had been bad ever since Little Jim came, and she had kept up by sheer force of will. A weaker woman would have given up to invalidism; but she was unwilling to allow any one to nurse the afflicted child, and her care for him took her mind off herself. It was his need of her that made her hurry back home, and her employment kept her from worrying as she would have done had she been idle.

It was a dreary ride for Maury Tallman. He took a seat in the Pullman, where he would be undisturbed, and he re-read Maxwell's letter and the clipping. More than it had done before, the letter appealed to him, and the ridicule of the correctness of the article, and criticism of the author, held out to him a faint hope that Maxwell was correct. His own feeling in the matter, however, was that Jim Miller would never have written his son-in-law such a letter without having what he considered absolute proof of the justness of his charge.

It was night when he arrived in the city; but Dr. Roberts was at home, and he answered the telephone himself, telling Maury to come right out to his residence. The interview was held in the same library where the Doctor had broken the news of the blindness of the baby to him.

"I am glad to see you again, Mr. Tallman. How are Mrs. Tallman and the baby?"

"Mrs. Tallman is not well; she has never regained her strength; but she seems better than she has been. The baby has never had a sick day. He is the happiest, best baby I ever saw."

"I am glad. And I hope your wife will be herself again soon."

Maury was calm and quiet. He had survived the first shock, and he had himself so well in hand that he was sure he could go through this interview without betraying his plans.

"Dr. Roberts," he said in a businesslike tone, "I have a few questions to ask you, and I am sure you will answer me frankly. I understand that ophthalmia neonatorium is responsible for nearly all the blindness of infants. You treated my child, and you know definitely whether that is the disease that destroyed his vision. Was it?"

"That is a direct question, Mr. Tallman, and I cannot afford to give you anything but a direct answer. I do not know where you got the technical term, but that is the cause of your baby's blindness."

"Thank you. Now, another question; is it a fact that that disease is the result of a specific germ conveyed to the eyes of the child by its mother at birth?"

"I see you have some definite knowledge of the matter, Mr. Tallman. I do not know why you want to know all this from me; but, as before, I can only answer in the affirmative."

"Very well. Is that germ the result of social sin?"

"Never, in all his experience, had the Doctor been so quizzed; nor had he ever known a layman to have such exact knowledge of the matter in hand. He realized the cold, clear questions of the business man, and he answered in the same clear fashion.

"It is."

"Is there any possible chance that my child was infected any other way?"

"Yes. It is possible to convey the disease on a towel, or in some other way. But that is not probable. You have asked me some plain questions, and I have answered them as plainly. You will, of course, allow me to make further statements regarding the matter."

"Yes. Tell me all. That is why I came to you."

If Dr. McConnel had opened the eyes of the father of the twins, Dr. Roberts let in the light of science on the subject to the banker, who sat before him that night. He could not understand the calm young father, who discussed the affliction of innocent women and children as he would have discussed a financial problem; but he knew he was relieving his own mind of a burden that had been on it for years. He told Maury of the many cases that were coming to him daily. Only that day, he had treated three babies suffering from this very trouble, and he was going to be able to save only one pair of little eyes.

"If I could have seen your child a week sooner, I might have saved it. I know I could have cured it during the first stages of the disease."

He wondered that the man who had chided himself before did not do so now; but Maury was not thinking of that. Under that calm exterior, the battle was beginning to rage again, and he was sure that he never could see the innocent victim of his own folly again.

"I thank you, Dr. Roberts," he said, as he arose to leave, "and I appreciate your frankness. All that you have told me ought to be told to the world, that this crime might come to an end. There are hundreds of men who would rather have their eyes put out than to marry and bring all this suffering and calamity on the innocent. We are ignorant criminals, but criminals, nevertheless."

Leaving the Doctor's residence, Maury returned to his hotel. Providing himself with stationery, and with a small vial, which he purchased at an all-night drug-store, he retired to his room to write the letter he had promised Jessie should reach her the next day.

That letter was too sacred for reproduction in these pages, but the one to Jim Miller is recorded, because it hurried the campaign the latter had decided on, and it shows the tortures through which this one awakened man passed as he paid the price he himself assessed for the folly of his youth.

"When I think of the happiness of your home before I entered it," he wrote, "and of the purity of your daughters before two moral lepers led them down the aisles of that stately church just two years ago, I feel like Satan must have felt when he saw Adam and Eve driven from the Garden of Eden. Some will say that I did not know I was doing wrong to marry Jessie, and I did not; others will say that there are hundreds that have done the same thing, and there are; but I sinned in sowing wild oats, and I must bear the penalty for all the consequences of my sowing. Indeed it was the wind—oh, what a fool I was! —and I reaped the whirlwind. You may blame me for what I am doing, and you may call it a rash act; but I can not look into little Jim's unseeing eyes, nor can I look into your clear ones. I am like Gehazi: the leprosy is on me because of my sin. I am like Cain: afraid to walk among men lest they see the mark on me and slay me. I am like Judas: I have betrayed innocent blood. Therefore, like Judas, I will end it all tonight.

"I leave all my property, real and personal, to Jessie, and I am glad there is enough to supply her needs of life, and to give Little Jim an education. Also I have set aside ten thousand dollars for you to handle as trustee. This amount I want you to use in enlightening the public on the evils of social sin. Use it in any way you may deem best. I believe, however, that there ought to be lectures delivered to the boys and girls in the grammar grades and high school grades of all our public schools on this question. If a county school physician was appointed in every county, whose duty it would be to visit each school in the county, and lecture on real physiology, and the laws of reproduction and sex hygiene, I am sure that the next generation would be saved untold misery, and that more could be accomplished than has been done for the race in the past thousand years. I almost wish I could live to see it.

"But enough. Forgive me, dear Mr. Miller. Forgive me. I remember our words the day you gave your consent to our marriage: 'I would not give her to a scrub.' But you did, though neither of us knew it at the time. Tell Mother Miller I am so sorry I have been a party to her grief and sorrow. Good-by. Think of me with as much charity as you can."

They found him the next morning. Rather, they found the cold form lying on the bed. There was a note to the management, directing that they wire Jim Miller at Tamalpias, and that he be given the letter addressed to him when he arrived. There was a letter of explanation to the coroner, and one to Maxwell Wright. He had mailed the letter to Jessie on a night train.

Only the angels know the anguish that had filled his heart as he lifted the deadly vial to his lips. There was no outward sign of struggle, nor mark of violence. He looked like one who had gone to sleep and forgotten to wake again.

The papers published sensational accounts of the suicide of a successful young banker, whose financial and domestic affairs were ideal, and speculated on the reason for the rash act. The reading public made surmises, and learned doctors gave opinion that it was dementia of some sort. Only Dr. Roberts and the dead man's relatives knew the real cause, and they kept their own counsel.

Again, Jessie took up her blind child and her burden of life, and entered the train. If she had suffered on that other trip, she experienced agony now. He had been with her then, and his anguish had eased hers. Now, he was gone, and she must bear it all alone. She had received the telegram early that morning, and his letter had come on the noon train. Forgetting her wasted strength, she had made hasty preparation and was on her way to her dead. His letter had told her of his remorse, and of the thousand deaths he had suffered since he had read Maxwell's letter and the clipping. Her grief was the keener that she had not been able to help him stand the terrible shock. How dreadful it must have been to face the thing alone! His act lost its criminal aspect to her; she could see nothing except a supreme evidence of his love for her and their afflicted baby. She saw him as a real martyr, and her love for him was crystalized into a sort of worship that she would carry through life.

Then, she thought of Allie, and of Maxwell Wright. What would the effect on him be? Instinctively, she knew that he would do nothing rash; but what would he do? Poor Allie! She had borne the curse and paid the penalty. But what was death to the curse she was bearing in her arms, in her diseased body, and in her breaking heart, as she hurried to the ghastly closing scene in the drama of two short years!

Jim Miller was himself surprised at the calm strength he found within him under the ordeal of this terrible climax to the marriage of the twins. His reserve force and tremendous willpower stood him in hand in this dark hour that made his loved ones lean so heavily on him. The incident only increased his determination to put himself into the fight for the race. He sought Dr. Roberts and made an engagement with him for the near future. His fight must be an intelligent one, and he was not going to spare time nor money.

The funeral was impressive. All Tamalpias was moved with sympathy. They did not know why Maury Tallman had killed himself, but they loved him, and their expressions of sorrow were sincere and eloquent.

It would be the hardest task of his life, but Jim Miller knew that he must tell the story of both tragedies in his coming campaign. Only hearts of stone would be able to resist the appeal he would be able to make, and that would be his compensation. He would sacrifice his timidity, and the sacredness of his sorrow, on the altar where his daughter had laid her life, his grandchild had given his eyes, another daughter her health, and his son-in-law had died in remorse. He tarried until the grave was filled; then, as the minister pronounced the benediction, he lifted his hand toward heaven and renewed the vow he had made at the riverside. Life, talent, time and money should be spent to emancipate the race from this plague that was so unnecessary and easily preventable.

His wife saw the uplifted hand and the moving lips, and knew what was passing. She pressed his left hand and whispered:

"You have come to the kingdom for such a time as this, and I am with you, Jim."

CHAPTER XIII.

JOHN PATTERSON.

Almost every Southern town has a character like John Patterson—a man above middle age, whose family once owned a large estate and many negroes; whose father reared him in idleness and supplied his purse with money, as well as having preached to him, and practised in his presence, the time-worn doctrine that a man has a perfect right to go to the devil if he wants to. Such a character, and John Patterson was no exception, always believed that the height of Southern aristocracy demands that he shall develop the ability to drink raw whiskey, and more of it than any other man in the community can drink, and still walk straight. He also learns to curse like a slave-driver, whether there is occasion for profanity or not, and he assumes a superior air in keeping with the number of slaves his family is reputed to have owned "before the wah." Go into his house and you will find old-fashioned furniture with faded upholstery, and a musty smell that fully warrants the claim that they are "among the oldest families of the State." This overbearing manner is only equaled by the presumption of the degenerate scion of a decadent aristocracy that makes him almost impudent in his intrusion on the affairs of others. He seems to think that the world owes him deference and a good living because of his antecedents. He resents the changes that have been wrought by reformers who have taken away his "personal liberty" by agitating the liquor question until the saloon has been voted out of the community, and he spends his time in cursing the reformers and dodging the officers on his way to the "blind tigers," where he can slake his thirst with an adulterated beverage branded "whiskey."

Generally, the family of such a character is proud and poor. They live on less than half the food they really need, and they spend money for clothes that ought to be spent for bread. They can do without food, but appearance can not be maintained without clothes. There is a negro family living in the "quarters" that partakes of this family pride far enough to look after their "white folks," and to do the laundry work. For this service, they get the cast-off clothing, free rent, and the opportunity to carry "scraps" from the kitchen. An old family horse, and a dilapidated surrey, a mangy dog, and an unkempt lawn, overgrown with rosebushes and cedars, complete the picture.

Every merchant in town has a bill that he would take five cents on the dollar for; but he continues to let the family have a few items occasionally, for several reasons. One of these is that the degenerate scion knows things that are better kept secret; another, that the merchant sometimes wants a favor that no one else can render, and still another that social position is at stake, and an ambitious wife importunes her husband to accommodate the proud family for her sake.

John Patterson and his wife possessed all these characteristics. He was tall and angular, with iron-gray hair, which was never combed; mustache and goatee to match; white shirt, ironed by the negro servant, with collar attached; black string tie, worn in a double bow; striped trousers that bagged at the knees; heavy shoes that were polished once a week at the barber-shop; black vest with only the bottom button in use, and a large white hat. His shaggy brows covered pale-gray eyes that peeped out at you when curious, swam, downcast, in tears when asking a favor, and blared, wide open, when defiant. And they were defiant when he was so thoroughly intoxicated that he began to give the history of his family, and tell of the negroes he would still own if it had not been for the accursed "Yankees" who were only jealous because they did not have the climate and employment that would enable them to keep negroes.

He always celebrated events of more than passing interest by getting drunk, when he could get the whiskey, and he generally got it some way. He succeeded in finding enough of it on the occasion of Maury Tallman's funeral to keep up his reputation for celebrating. His need must have been great, for it was the first time he had ever pawned or sold anything that became a matter of public knowledge; but, this time, the owner of a suspicious livery stable went to Patterson's barn and led away the old brown mare that had pulled the family surrey ever since John had returned to Tamalpias with his wife and the boy, Drury.

Perhaps it was the quantity, and it may have been partially due to the quality, that the celebration took on the proportions of a protracted spree. At any rate, more than a week went by, and he was still drinking and delivering lectures to any one who would listen, about the "good old times when everybody had a decanter on his mantel, and a gentleman could have a little fun without being considered a fool." His wife was distressed about him, and had Mose, the negro man who lived in the cabin, watch him and keep him out of trouble.

Drury came home from school when the spree was almost two weeks old, and, when he tried to control his father, the old man railed on him, and called him a "brat," and told him to keep his place. It was the first time Drury had ever been talked to like that, and he was deeply wounded. He appealed to his mother, and she cried and shook her head.

"It is the worst he has ever been," she said. "I have lived with him more than twenty years, but he would always listen to me before; now, he curses me, and charges me with his ruin. I am afraid his mind is unbalanced."

"I know it is, Mother. His brain is burned out by alcohol, and he will get worse. I am going to stay with you as long as he lives. Where did he get so much liquor?"

"Jim Davis sold it to him for the little mare."

"I wish we could prove that; it would send him to prison."

John Patterson became more unruly, and the city marshall told Drury he would have to be kept off the streets. That was hard to do; but Mose and Drury got him home, and locked him in a room. Finding himself a prisoner, he became furious, and smashed the furniture and broke the windows. They dared not get within his reach, for there was murder in his eye. At last, they sent for Dr. McConnell, and he saw his patient was showing symptoms of delirium tremens again. He began a treatment; but, that night, John Patterson was a screaming, kicking, fighting maniac. It took four men to hold him in his bed. Although Drury had seen men brought to the medical school with "snakes," nothing like this had come under his observation. Could it be possible that this writhing, frothing, demented being was his father! Was this demon in his veins, lying dormant, only awaiting a propitious time for a sudden attack on his manhood? His brain reeled with the crushing knowledge that the children of drunkards are handicapped for life in the estimation of the world, and in the fact that they inherit the depraved appetites and passions of their ancestors. He had just begun to study heredity, and he resolved, as he looked at his maniacal father, possessed with a thousand demons, that he would go to the bottom of this grave question. No matter where it led him, nor what the consequences were, he must know the truth. If there was any chance that he would in any way blight the happiness of the girl he loved through his inheritance from this man, he would never marry her. His heart chilled at the thought, and his face bespoke the agony that even the suggestion caused him.

Jim Miller went to see John Patterson for a double purpose: to offer any assistance he might be able to render, and to study the case closely. His investigations had already shown him that the campaign he was planning had to do with the question of this dissipation as well as the other, and he wanted to see for himself the final effects of such a life as John Patterson had lived. When he entered the room, the poor man was struggling with his attendants, and yelling:

"Let me go! He'll get me. Don't you see him there behind that tree? Oh! He shot me. Let me go, let me go. Look, he has divided himself into ten devils, and they are all grinning at me. Oh, quit licking out that fiery tongue at me!"

Thus he raved for three hours. When the Doctor tried to give him medicine with a spoon, he bit the spoon and twisted the handle almost in two. He scratched himself and tore his clothing into shreds. Once, he caught sight of Drury, and he shouted at him:

"Get out of here, you fool! Don't stand there looking at me with those accusing eyes. You look exactly like he did the night of the fire. I see you trying to choke me. Put him out; he wants to kill me. Put him out, I say."

The fact that his father was suffering the

tortures of mental delusion did not take all the sting out of the words for Drury. There must be something in the subconscious mind of the man to make him speak like this at sight of the young man. His wonder increased as Mrs. Patterson, overhearing the words of the madman, rushed into the room and put her arms around him as if to shield him from the fury of her husband.

"John," she cried, "what are you saying! Drury, my child, come with me. He is wild, and does not know what he is saying," and she led him from the room.

"It is only a wild fancy of his disordered brain. Don't let it disturb you, Son. Twice, while you have been away. he has had these attacks; but he is much worse this time than ever before. You do not know what I have suffered these recent years, since he began to drink more than he could walk erect with. His early drinking made him act dignified, and he was never more kind than when in his cups. But during the last five years, he has grown rougher and more inconsiderate."

"When did he begin drinking, Mother?"

"Before I met him. He says he drank from his earliest recollection. and he used to try to feed you 'toddy' with a spoon; but you never did like it."

"I have been much worried for fear I would some day develop the appetite for drink, by inheritance from him."

"No. no, my boy, you need never fear that.

You are in no more danger in that way than I am."

"But mother, science teaches that the child does inherit such things from the parent."

"You will never have trouble with drink on his account; if you form the habit, it will be your own fault. I know what I am saying. Let whiskey alone and it will let you alone."

Drury saw she was under restraint and wondered. He had noticed this demeanor in his mother every time the subject of his looks or his ways was discussed. He would have pressed the matter; but she changed the subject, and he was soon called into the sick-room again.

Jim Miller heard John Patterson rave at the boy. and he. too, wondered what he could mean. The words were full of mystery to him, and to Dr. McConnell. There had been no fire at Tamalpias that he could be referring to, yet Jim was sure there was some connection between the raving of the madman and a real occurrence. This opinion was strengthened when Drury came into the room again, and was soon recognized by the sufferer. This time, however, the old man cowered and tried to pull the cover over his head. He moaned piteously, and begged for mercy.

"Don't hurt me; I had to do it. All the devils were pulling at me, and one stuck out his tongue at me and cursed me. He made me do it. Go away, go away, and let me get on the boat. There he is! He's going to choke me! There they all come. Fire! Fire!" And it took all their strength to hold him in the bed.

After that, he settled down and spoke no more. His struggles were over, and only the twitching of the muscles indicated the pain that racked his body. Darkness filled the room, but a greater gloom filled the hearts of mother and son as they were told the end had come. It was relief to both; nevertheless, their sorrow was great.

The same spirit that gave the drunkard recognition during life caused the citizenship to give him a funeral that would have shown honor to a more worthy person. The floral offerings were numerous, expensive, and beautiful. The casket was the best to be had, and the two lodges to which the deceased had belonged, turned out in full regalia. With true Southern charity, they buried John Patterson's imperfections, and his debts, with him. His virtues were extolled, and his vices were too well known to need mentioning. The few old comrades that were there resolved to quit drinking, and went straight back to town and hunted up some liquor to cheer them up a little.

The widow and the son found the Millers real friends in this dark hour. They well knew that those who were conspicuous at the funeral would be the last to help them in the coming days, and it warmed their hearts to have these good people show genuine sympathy that would endure when the parade was over. Mr. Harris and his family said a kind word or two; but Mrs. Patterson knew it would be only a few days until she would be forced to give up her home on account of the mortgage her husband had given Mr. Harris.

Thus John Patterson died: bankrupt, ruined, demented, home gone, family disgraced, friends alienated, soul lost—all for a mess of pottage!

CHAPTER XIV.

AN OLD CLIPPING.

Several months had passed by, and the events recorded in the last two chapters were history that had been discussed in Tamalpias until there was nothing more to be said. Jessie Tallman had returned from Sharman, and had succeeded in purchasing the cottage Maury had built to take his bride to. Little Jim was walking and talking, and was the idol of all the relatives. He was really a bright child, and Jessie was already in correspondence with a governess who had been recommended by the superintendent of the State school for the blind.

Jim Miller had been busy gathering data for his campaign, which was to begin in the early summer. He had become more convinced than ever of the righteousness and correctness of the cause he had resolved to champion. His wife, too, had entered into the matter with him, and she was planning to make tours over the State and speak to women under the auspices of the White Ribboners. Jack had finished his high school course and was away at college. Dixie would graduate at Barlow within two months; then, she was going to keep house while her mother was away. Jessie would stay with her, and the arrangement was considered ideal.

Drury Patterson had taken his mother with him when he returned to school. They were doing light housekeeping, and finding it a happy solution of their trouble. The old home had been sold to satisfy the mortgage, and Mr. Harris had purchased it and deeded it to Marvin, who rejoiced that he had superseded Drury in one thing at any rate.

Jim Miller employed a foreman for his ranch, who could take entire charge of all his affairs in that line, and announced in the local papers that he was a candidate for the State senate. His opponent was a man that had been brought up in politics; he was recognized as the political boss of that district, and would have the "ring" at his beck and call. Bill Colton was also an unscrupulous trickster; he could win the election if his opponent was an ordinary reformer; for he could talk reforms as well as anybody. It was one thing to talk reforms, and another to enact them into laws.

Thus things stood when Dixie Miller came home with her diploma from Barlow College. Trouble, experience, and hard work had ripened her, but had not robbed her of the freshness and beauty of her girlhood. Marvin Harris had been paying court to Thelma Dawson for nearly two years; but he could not resist the winsome beauty who had been his playmate and little sweetheart. He had learned many things about courting a girl since his beginning with Dixie, three years before, and he was sure he could win her love, now that Drury was so far away.

He had settled down to business, and everybody was praising him for his unquestionable ability. He had remodeled the Patterson place, and it was now the prettiest residence in the whole town. The superintendent of the city schools had rented it, and Dixie had to admit that it was a wonderful example of civic improvement. Also, she saw that the improvement in the owner was greater than in his property. He was handsome and refined, and he acted like a getleman. She had always admired Mr. Harris, and Marvin was growing more like his father every day.

Dixie was unpacking her trunks and destroying the letters and papers that had accumulated during her college course. There were letters from Allie, and some from other relatives and friends that she could not bring herself to destroy. Drury's letters were neatly arranged in a box and chronologically filed; she counted them among her dearest possessions, and they were placed back in the tray of a trunk. She had finished feeding the flames on the hearth, and was rising from her position on the floor, when she saw a scrap of paper that had escaped her. She unfolded it and was surprised to discover that it was the article she had clipped from a magazine two years before. It was the one she had read on the train, and dealt with the subject of alcoholism. Almost involuntarily, she sat down and re-read it. If it had shocked her before, it scared her now; for she saw a new meaning in it that had not dawned on her at the first reading. She had thought only of the effect of inheritance on Drury: now, she saw the fearful truth that two more generations were at stake. Like a phantom, the words of the Mosaic Law arose before her. "Thy God is a jealous God, visiting the iniquities of the fathers upon the children unto the third and fourth generation of them that hate Me." Was it possible that the immediate generation might escape the penalty, only to be the means of passing the curse on to the next? Her father would know, and she hurried down-stairs to ask him about it.

"Daddy, I am coming back to you with this old question of heredity. Please read this treatise and then tell me what I want to know."

He read it in the light of the investigations he had been making for more than a year, and his heart went out to his child. He knew what her question would be, and he was pained at the answer he must give.

"Tell me, Daddy, is it possible that one generation may escape this appetite, and then it develop in the next?"

"My child, I see what you are thinking, and I must tell you the truth: my reading leads me to believe that the predispositions, passions, and appetites are more likely to show up in alternate generations than in the immediate. I may be wrong about this, but I shall write to Dr. Chadwick L. Grady, the great alienist, and ask him about it. Meantime, I hope you will not worry over this question."

"I can not help worrying. If there is a possibility that Mr. Patterson's appetite may be imparted to his grandchild through his son, can you not see what it means to me? Oh, this cruel world! And to think that men will claim they have a right to go on in their sin, when they are entailing such things on unborn generations. What punishment! And the innocent have to suffer for the crimes of the guilty!"

"Yes, Dixie, it is terrible. No one knows how terrible, better than I. Think how it has come to my family; and this blow to you, if I am correct in my judgment, is also a blow to me. I love the boy, and really wanted him to marry you. We must not forget him, either. If this thing is true, it makes him an Ishmaelite; he is too high principled ever to marry if he knows this curse is in his veins."

"You are right, Father. He said almost as much to me when his father died. How can we ever stand it!"

"Don't give up, daughter, until I hear from Dr. Grady. I shall put the whole case before him, and we will abide by his decision, will we not?"

That short question put her love in the balance against her intellect. Love cried out for its object in spite of opinions, science, and consequences. More rebellion than she had ever suspected her heart held, surged within her being. She threw herself on a couch and sobbed. Intellect prompted her to yield natural selection to wisdom and scientific fact; but love was slow to go to the altar of sacrifice.

Jim took her hand and knelt by her side. His grief was as great as hers, and he felt some of the rebellion that was making the battle so hard for her. Nevertheless, he knew wisdom would win, and he dealt very gently with this third daughter of his who was suffering on account of the sins of others. He did not underestimate the suffering, nor discount its reality.

"Dixie, darling, yours is a peculiar sorrow. Your lover is personally worthy, and there is no reason for your love, or his, to be conquered. By the decrees of an All-wise Creator, you can not possess each other. And it is the best thing for the race that these evils be curtailed rather than perpetuated through offspring. Be brave my girl. That is right; I knew you would be sensible."

"Oh, it is so hard to do! But I will abide by the decision of Dr. Grady. Write to him at once, and let me know, as quickly as you can, what he says."

"You are a noble girl, Dixie, and I believe that God will reward you in some way for this great sacrifice."

It was ten days before the answer came from Dr. Grady. Jim was in his office, down-town, when he opened and read the letter.

"In compliance with your request," the Doctor wrote, "I beg to reply that the general doctrine of hereditary influence has been recognized since the days of mythology. The nervous condition of the parents endows the future child with their general characteristics and predispositions. The child of a drunkard starts out under unfavorable conditions, and in all its after life can not entirely escape the consequences, physical and mental, that have been entailed on it by the condition of its parent.

"Much attention and thought should be given this great question. At the present time, insane people, drunkards, epileptics, cancerous, scrofulous, and all kinds of diseased people propagate and perpetuate their imperfections without a word being said against it.

"As to one generation escaping the appetite for stimulants, and the next generation developing it, allow me to say that such cases are on record. A son may inherit enough will-power from his mother, and have such effective training, that he will overcome the latent desire for drugs or intoxicants, but the child of such a son seems to have intensified thirst, and sooner or later yields to the call of his ancestry. I have no record of a child entirely void of the appetite where the father was a drinker before the birth of the child, as in the case you cite, but I am sure such a case is possible. The sure course is for your daughter not to marry the young man in question."

This corroboration of his judgment did not stun the father as much as did the fact that he must tell his child that science had decreed that she must never marry the man she loved so well. It would also become his duty to break the news to Drury. He dreaded that even more than telling Dixie, because she was somewhat prepared for the cruel news.

When he went home that afternoon, he led Dixie into the library and handed her the letter to read. He expected another outburst of grief, but she did not cry out. Her sobs were deep; however, the storm had passed, and she accepted the decision as a foregone conclusion.

"You will write to Drury?" she asked, as she handed the letter back to him.

"Yes."

"Write at once, and I shall write as soon as he has had time to get your letter."

She started from the room, but came back and stood by his chair.

"Daddy," she said, stroking his hair, "I knew what news this letter would bring, and I have been planning my future. I shall enter a sanatorium and become a trained nurse. I can not spend my life in luxury and idleness, and I can be of so much service to the world as a nurse."

"O child, I am afraid I can never consent to that. Think it over, and let me study about it a while. Am I to lose my last daughter from my home? Give me time to study it all out before you speak of this to any one else."

"I will, but my own mind is made up. I know you will see it as I do. My life must be too busy for recollection."

Then, she left him and went to her room.

Drury was in New Orleans when he received Jim Miller's letter that condemned him to a bachelor's life. It was the kindest letter he had ever received, and the writer reassured him of his friendship and confidence. He invited him to come to his home and see Dixie whenever he wished; but he made it plain that, in the light of the very science Drury was studying, he could never marry Dixie. The blow was heavy; it was as if he stood again looking at his father dying under the influence of torturing demons. Not only the loss of the woman he hoped to marry, but the stigma it cast on him made him groan under the cross that was laid on his young shoulders. The walls and the furniture about him seemed to cry out:

"You are the child of a drunkard. There's poison in your veins. You are unfit to be a husband and father. You are an Ishmaelite."

He would not tell his mother. She had recovered from the shock of her husband's death, and her health was much improved; however, he could not bring himself to tell her he had been condemned because he was John Patterson's child. She must be spared the pain that knowledge would bring her.

The next day, he received a letter from Dixie, and it was balm to his wounded soul. She revealed her suffering, and told him frankly of her abiding love. Then, she told him of her purpose to become a trained nurse, and urged him to go to the top in his profession. If they could not marry, they could at least give their lives to the relief of human misery. They might even work together in the same hospital, some day. She asked him to come to see her shortly, and they would talk it over together.

Of course, Marvin Harris did not go to Dr. McConnell's office with the intention of eavesdropping; it is also true that he did not leave when he began to overhear the conversation between Jim Miller and the Doctor. They were in the Doctor's private room and Marvin was in the waiting-room; but the transom was open and he could hear every word. Jim was telling the old Doctor of the letter he had received from Dr. Grady, and of the decision he and Dixie had come to in regard to Drury Patterson. The listener's face grew red; then, a gratified smile wreathed his face. He was becalmed, however, when he heard Mr. Miller tell the physician that Dixie had decided to enter a hospital for training as a nurse, and he had given his consent.

Marvin slipped out of the room and down to the street. This was the best news he had ever heard. Even if she went away for training, she would yet be his wife. Although he was engaged to Thelma Dawson, that was a small matter. He laughed as he thought of honest, clean, temperate Drury Patterson being turned down because he was the child of a drunkard. He, himself, had drunk more whiskey than Drury ever had, and he had "gone the gaits," but he was the child of a gentleman. It was just as he had told her, and it was all working out better than he had dared to hope. However, he must be diplomatic in his endeavor to win her. She was as strong in character as she was beautiful in person, and he had blundered before.

There was to be a social event of first importance next week, and he wrote her that afternoon, asking the pleasure of her company. She did not want to attend the function; but her father's cause demanded the presence of the family, and she did not see any reason why she should not accept the company of such a gentleman as Marvin was proving himself to be; so his delight was supreme when he read her note of formal acceptance.

It was her first public appearance, and she aroused the envy of the women and the admiration of the men to the highest pitch. Her reticent manner only added to her charms, and the dignity lent her by her great purpose in life gave her the bearing of a colonial lady. She was just gracious enough to escape criticism, and reserved enough to call forth the deepest respect. Jim Miller had never been as proud of one of his children as he was of her on this occasion, and her mother's hopes were realized. Jessie told her afterward that she was the most lovely creature she had ever seen.

"But that is not what I want to be, Jessie, I want to be the most useful girl this town has ever given to the world," and she meant it with all her heart.

Marvin was disappointed because he could not bring himself to be sentimental with this dignified girl. When he tried to be the least bit gallant, she was as cold as ice. He asked permission to call on her at home; but she gave him a little smile and said:

"It isn't worth while, Marvin. I am going to leave for Chilton within a few weeks. It hasn't been given out yet, but I am going to be a trained nurse."

"I thought you and Drury were going to marry?"

"Your thoughts were premature."

There, he had blundered again; for there was that in her simple words that prematurely dismissed the subject.

What he failed to say to her in speech that night, he wrote the next day. His declaration was manly and simple. He begged her to dismiss the idea of becoming a nurse, and to give him a chance to win her love. He was not in a hurry, and, if she would go away for training, he begged the privilege of writing her occasionally.

Her answer was polite and definite. She told him that she would never marry, and that it would be a waste of time, and altogether futile for him to write her with the hope that she would alter her decision. She thanked him for the honor conferred, and wished him all happiness and success. So thoroughly did she dispose of the matter that he went back to Miss Dawson, and, very soon thereafter, their engagement was announced. Dixie could not repress a smile when she heard the news the day before she left Tamalpias.

Drury came that afternoon. Never had he undertaken a task so difficult. He felt that everybody in Tamalpias knew of his plight, and, while he was sure of Jim Miller's confidence and sympathy, he could not repress the feeling that he was an intruder, an outcast among men. Mr. Miller soon put him at his ease. Dixie was the same sweet woman, and the love-light in her gray eyes told him that, to her, he was a man among his fellows. Mrs. Miller treated him as a son, and Jessie and Jack made him know that he was at home and honored for his own sake.

His work had won for him appointment as interne at the very hospital where Dixie had secured admittance as an apprentice, and this modified their mutual sorrow. Drury had made his own investigations, and thoroughly coincided with the decision of the Millers that marriage was out of the question. He expressed his appreciation of the fact that Jim Miller had kept the matter confidential, except that he had told Dr. McConnell.

The two years and more of almost entire absence from Tamalpias had brought Drury to manhood, and a type of manhood that pleased his friends very much. He was larger than they had expected him to be, and his touch with great teachers had given him a breadth and equilibrium that made one feel there was a future for the young doctor; and it made him just a little vain to have old schoolmates use the title so naturally and with real deference. He even dreamed of a day when he could come back and prove his right to the appellation by taking up practice among them.

Dr. McConnell renewed his urgent invitation for Drury to finish his time as interne and enter partnership with him, and clinched the invitation with the argument that a couple of years of general practice would the better prepare him for the successful practice of surgery; and Drury was so convinced that he entered into the compact.

The visit was a pleasant one for Drury, and would have been without regret had it not been for a dark insinuation from Marvin Harris on the day of his departure. It was not what he said, but the implied meaning of his words made Drury know that his enemy either knew, or suspected, the real status of matters between him and Dixie. He was glad to get away from it all, and out into the busy world, where he could settle down to the task he had set himself. Dixie had gone on two days before, and they would be an inspiration to each other.

CHAPTER XV.

THE FIRST CAMPAIGN.

American politics has degenerated to the point where men, instead of issues, are the controlling factors. No matter what the issue may be in local, State, or National elections, the side or party wins that has the greatest leader. A strong personality, ability to talk loud and long, and plenty of money will elect any man or carry any cause in almost any section of the country. The result is that clean, self-respecting men keep out of the game, and statesmanship is becoming a rare thing. When the politicians have become so corrupt that a suffering public can stand the graft and slavery no longer, a reform movement is started, there is scandal, and a few men are punished for the crimes of the system. The newspapers print sensational stories of corruption and graft, then declare that there has been a civic reform that will make the repetition of the same thing impossible. The people swell with pride and swagger back to their homes, offices, and business only to relapse into their former lethargy, while a new set of gangsters takes the place of the old and finishes out the interrupted game of personal politics for the spoils of public office and public funds.

Thus it is an endless round of corruption and graft, exposure, and reform. Nor will it ever be different until the whole system is purged, and real merit and ability are recognized and rewarded.

Nowhere is all this truer than in those offices where the salaries and fees are inadequate to support an honest man who is capable of the service that is to be rendered. Representatives and State senators are paid such small salaries that very few men who are worthy and able to legislate, can be induced to leave their own affairs to serve the public. It is also a fact that, when a few such men are patriotic enough to sacrifice their own interests in order to try to pass some needed laws, they find the legislative halls crowded with men who have "pull," and the affairs of state overshadowed by the lowest type of personal politics.

Jim Miller had not gone far in his campaign until he learned all this. At first, it made the outlook gloomy for him, and he was somewhat discouraged. Bill Colton had the best of him in experience, ability to harangue the voters, and the fact that he was one of the Governor's henchmen. It was only the magnitude of his cause that made him set his jaws and determine to fight to the last ditch against the monster that had brought death and ruin to his family. He soon saw that his hope lay in enlightening the masses on the evils he sought to stamp out. To that end, he had printed thousands of circulars and booklets giving the facts he had learned and the evidence he had gathered. He spoke timidly at first, but soon found his liberty, and, by the time he had been on the hustings two weeks, he was drawing great crowds by his burning eloquence. He had not intended referring to his sorrows; but, under the spell of his enthusiasm, he finally told the story of Allie's death and little Jim's blindness as the results of the profligate lives of the men who had married his daughters. He was not bitter, his sorrow had softened him toward those ignorant men; his heart was broken, and even his enemies could see that he was making an appeal rather than uttering condemnation. His purpose was so unselfish, and his object so humanitarian that he drew to his support the intelligent voters who usually shrank from active part in politics. Teachers, doctors, and ministers rallied to him, and the plain farmers and ranchers were aroused from their indifference to champion this new leader, who proposed to emancipate their daughters and sisters from the curse of a double standard.

Bill Colton reported to the corruptionists that his opponent had attacked the liquor traffic and was using scientific evidence to show its hereditary effects. He called on them to get contradictory statements from doctors and ministers, and to send him money to keep this agitator out of the legislature. The money was forthcoming by return mail, and he had assurance that literature would reach him immediately that would offset the work of the "fanatic" that was trying to prejudice the mind of the public against their business.

Nor was he disappointed. There will always be men in the medical professon, and in the ministry, that can be hired to make statements intended to shield wrong-doers and bad business.

The district was soon flooded with circulars denying the truth Jim was teaching, and they had the appearance of authentic opinions by physicians and ministers.

They had reckoned without their host, however; for Jim Miller was quick to send detectives to locate every man whose name was on these circulars. Their main medical authority was found to be a man that had really taken a course in medicine, but had become a slave to the cocaine habit, and would do anything to get the drug. One of the ministers had been excluded from the church, and was a cobbler, and a lecturer on Socialism. Thus it went with the lot. Neither side spared money nor printer's ink. The women took up the fight, and no such campaign had ever been waged, not even the prohibition campaign of five years before, as swept that senatorial district when Jim Miller ran for the office on behalf of pure manhood and character, and Bill Colton ran in the interests of liquor, libertinism, and dirty politics.

Colton's crowd sent men to Kentucky in an endeavor to find something in Jim Miller's past history that would help them in their failing cause; but there was nothing to be uncovered that would help defeat him. His record was clean all the way through, and he had always been honest and straightforward in his dealings with men, and they abandoned that effort. In vain, they urged his lack of political influence and knowledge of law and law-making. Jim replied that he did not claim much of either; but he did know that something must be done. It was money, place, and liquor against women and babies. He had contributed children and a grandchild, and was now giving time and money on the side of innocent human beings; let those who would have protection for coming generations vote for him, and Bill Colton and his crowd must bear the responsibility of their position.

People are slow to learn, and the magnitude of the task Jim Miller had set for himself made many sympathize with him, then shake their heads and prophesy failure. Some were horrified at public discussion of such delicate matters and condemned Jim for agitating them. These prudes were of both sexes and of all ages. They held up their hands in holy horror as they declared it an outrage that such sacred things should be dragged into politics. Colton caught at this straw and made much of it. He deplored the decadence of gentility that suffered men to so excite women that they would leave their firesides to dabble in questions that were proper to be discussed only in the office of a physician.

Jim found, also, that when you raise the question of curtailing a man's natural propensities, however depraved they may be, you have at once aroused the opposition of that man. His proposed laws were construed to mean that certain personal rights and liberties were to be taken from men, and they resented the idea. Young men congregated in the pool-halls and loafing-places, and discussed the proposition that every man would have to get a certificate from two physicians declaring him fit before he could get a license to wed. They were against that; for they found it was true that not more than one out of five of them could get such certificates. He was also proposing a law that no man could get a license to wed who had been intoxicated twice in the preceding twelve months. They could not stand for that!

Some of his friends began to fear that there was danger of his being assassinated by a drink-crazed partisan who considered his rights were at stake. But Jim Miller was not a coward, nor was he intimidated by idle threats. He answered all their arguments with logic and the most withering sarcasm. When asked what he would do in the event Colton defeated him, he replied instantly:

"I would make the race again, two years hence. But I am not going to be defeated. My fight is righteous and unselfish, and I am going to win. Watch the returns."

It was sure to be a close race. Colton was claiming the district by a large majority; but that is a trick of the politicians. Miller was saying little and working hard right up to the last moment. The women had organized over the whole district, and, on election day, they met in the churches early in the morning and spent the entire day in praying that their champion would win. This was counterbalanced by jugs of whiskey hidden in barns and old store buildings, to which the thirsty voter was piloted by one of Colton's workers.

The weather was fine and the voting heavy. Jim Miller stayed in his office at Tamalpias, where he could keep in touch with the situation by telephone. Before noon, there began to be reports from certain places that Mexicans and negroes were being voted in squads by Colton's men. It was too late to help it; but, in case of a close vote, it might furnish ground for a contest. Jim instructed his men at other places to look out for the same trick and prevent it if possible. As reports of coercion and corruption came in on the one hand, and of work and prayers and tears on the other, he was reminded of the battle that was waged over the unconscious form of Allie. His chin quivered and his breath came in gasps. Then, he clenched his teeth and struck the table with his first, as he muttered:

"I must win! To lose this fight is to lose my revenge for the wrongs of my children. O Allie, my child, I must win!"

The returns came in slowly. Now, Miller was ahead; then, it was Colton. Through the night, it was first one then the other in the lead. The unofficial count gave Colton five votes majority. There followed a week of uneasy waiting for the official count to be announced. No contests were filed, and the commissioner's report would be final. On the strength of the reports by telephone and mail, Bill Colton and his crowd got drunk and shouted over their victory. Bill showed a roll of bills that he had saved for himself out of the slush fund sent him by outside interests.

Their rejoicing came to a sudden and timely

end when it was announced that Jim Miller had carried the district by fifty-seven votes. Then, the other camp began to rejoice and send tokens to each other. Congratulations came to Jim from over the whole State and from other States. His wife and Jessie had helped him more than they knew, and he told them so that night.

"But this is only the first skirmish; we have yet to fight the real battle. What they have done here is only an indication of the fight the opposition will put up in the legislature. My consolation lies in the fact that, while the battle rages, the people are being enlightened. Maury was right; we must educate the young, and I am going to urge the passage of laws that will give to every county a school physician whose duty it will be to lecture to the boys in the grammar and high-school grades on these subjects. Then, I want a lady with medical training to lecture to the girls in the same grades on sex hygiene and physiology. Education is the only way out, after all."

"Yes," agreed his wife, "I am sure you are right, and I want to establish a school for the training of these lady lecturers. The ten thousand dollars Maury set aside for this purpose will be a nucleus, and we can add to it. I have been thinking that, perhaps, this is the work Dixie can help us inaugurate after she has finished her training."

"That is capital!" cried Jim, and they fell to planning to complete their revenge on the Monster that had devoured their former happiness.

Jessie was as enthusiastic as her parents in the undertaking, and asked to be allowed a part in it. Her income was sufficient to enable her to give both time and money to it, and her father gladly accepted her offer. If Jack and Dixie joined them, and they would, the whole family would be arrayed in the war against the giant wrong.

"Senator" Miller, as his fellow citizens now called him, did not wait until the legislature convened to push the campaign of enlightenment. He continued to gather information and data, and publish circulars and tracts by the thousands. He established a paper in the interests of the movement and secured one of the best editorial managers and writers in the country to take charge of it. Purity journals and magazines throughout the Nation recognized a hero had come to the front, and tendered him their assistance. Other States took cognizance of the movement, and the obscure ranchman had started a wave of real reform that was destined to move surely, though slowly, until his revenge would be complete.

As he expected, he found opposition of the most formidable kind awaiting him at the Capitol. But the fiercest opposition was not as much in his way as the type of personal politics we have referred to. From janitor to Governor, every man was only a cog in a wheel that revolved round a Boss who marked the destiny of men and measures as a shipping clerk checks the articles on his bills. His proposed bills would have to be stamped "O. K." by this Boss before they could pass, and he was not long in finding out that the Boss was against any measure that struck, even indirectly, at moral questions. When he became satisfied that he could not secure the enactment of his bills during that term, he threw himself into other matters with a vim and wisdom that made the politicians sit up and take notice that the new Senator was out of the ordinary, and would have to be taken into account. He was sure of a second term, according to the custom of his party in the State, and he could afford to work another two years to attain his end.

The Boss tried to approach him, and his colleagues hinted at the advantage there was in being on good terms with the Boss. They tried coercion when other tactics failed; but Jim Miller could not see why men elected by the people should have a Boss, and he told them so in open debate. Although he did not realize it at the moment, he was throwing down the gauntlet to the Boss, and that individual proceeded to pick it up at once. That was the beginning. The end is not yet.

CHAPTER XVI.

THE HOUSE OF HEALING.

It was born in the heart of a man—this House of Healing. The man's friend had died for want of surgical attention, and the man dreamed of a sanitarium where other men could have the very best service possible. He bided his time, studying the question and planning, visiting hospitals, talking with surgeons, and gathering money. He sent his architects to Baltimore and New York with instructions to make plans for a building that would be ideal for its great purpose. Then, through the months on months consumed in the erection, he watched the materials brought in and put together. The groans of those mangled by cars and trucks on the streets of his city found an echo in his heart, and he urged the contractors to hurry. His first thought, as he opened his eyes each morning, was of the House of Healing, and he would look out of his east window to see if the walls were yet high enough to be discovered over the intervening house-tops. Many moonlight nights he walked amid the shadows of naked steel beams that were slowly finding their places for floors and elevator shafts. Architects put it on paper, artisans carried out the instructions of the blue-prints, quarries and mines yielded up their treasure to furnish the materials; but the building was conceived and born of this man's heart. He experienced all the anguish of travail as it came into being, and his hand patted its corridors, and caressed its pillars, as tenderly as any mother ever kissed her first-born.

At last, it was finished. The doctors came, and the nurses. White beds filled the wards and rooms. Appliances, instruments, tables, were in place. Washed, medicated air passed through it, warmed or cooled according to the thermostats set by the attendants. Elevators ran noiselessly up and down, and the patients began to arrive. The House of Healing was absolutely fire-proof and sanitary. The man looked on, and the first smile, since his friend had died, lighted his noble face. The child was full-grown and beginning to serve an afflicted race. Why should not the man show his gratification by a smile? Generation after generation will be served in the House of Healing, and the name of the man will be spoken after he has taken his last farewell of the child of his heart This is real life.

It was to this magnificent institution that Dixie went for training, and in which Drury had the good fortune to be appointed interne. They saw little of each other except on the occasion of holidays, or the chance meeting in one of the operating rooms, or in a charity ward. Both had passed the purely sentimental stage, and their environment and their purpose in life precluded any silly happenings in their relationships.

Drury became a general favorite with students and doctors, and showed natural adaptability and aptitude. He loved surgery and was soon kept busy assisting in emergency cases. The Man came to notice him, and gave him much encouragement by his kindly words; Drury loved the Man at once and wished to be like him. Nor did he wish in vain; for it was soon whispered that he looked like the Man, and his voice unconsciously partook of the quality of the Man's. He walked like the Man, and, most of all, he wanted to be the character this Man evidently was.

Dixie was quick to notice the change in him, and as quick to locate the ideal after which he was moulding his life. She was glad, too. Everybody loved the Man, and many tried to imitate him, and made themselves ridiculous in the attempt. However, Drury was not trying to imitate him, and would have been insulted by the suggestion. He simply wanted to be like him in character, and was unconsciously acting and speaking like him on that account. Although his fellows noticed it, they refrained from twitting him, as they did the others, because they knew he was guileless in the matter.

Several months had passed by when Drury and Dixie had a half-holiday together. They went to a beautiful park for a few hours, and Dixie told him of her father's election, and the plans of the family. His interest was keen, and he expressed his approval of the idea of a school of training for woman lecturers in the public schools.

"You will make an ideal principal of such a school, Dixie. Since I can not make a home for you, I shall be glad to see you make your life count in that way."

"That is the only compensation I can ever hope to have. Otherwise, I should not care to live."

"Are you not finding pleasure in your service here?"

"Yes, indeed. I want to tell you! The sweetest thing happened a few days ago. They brought in that little urchin, you remember, that had been run over by a motorcycle? Well, after the doctors had finished the operation, I was put in charge of his case. There was a small room on my floor not in use, and the head nurse directed that he be put in there. It was quite a while before he recovered from the effects of the anesthetic, and he went to sleep without seeming to notice anything. Late in the afternoon, I was sitting by his bedside when he awoke. He looked at me, then at the white bed, at the walls and furniture, and at some white roses in a vase. Then, he turned to me and said: 'O yes, I know. It killed me, and I am in heaven, and you are God's wife!' Poor child, he had never been on a clean bed before, did not even know that such a place as the House of Healing existed on earth."

"You must tell the Man about that."

"I did. It was the first time I have ever seen tears in his eyes. Isn't he grand!"

"Indeed he is. I wish I was one-third as good as he."

"You are, my dear boy. You must remember he has had many years to ripen that character in, and you will be just as fine and grand as he, at that age."

"In your eyes, I hope at least."

"Yes, and in goodness and usefulness to the world."

Then, they wandered about the park, feeding the squirrels, and watching the fish in the fountain, until time to return to their duties.

If Dixie found little romances and happy incidents in her work, she also found things not so pleasant. Sometimes, her patient would be a grouchy old man, who could never be pleased nor humored. Again, there would be a querulous old woman, who would persist in talking when told to be quiet; or a stubborn boy, who would not obey. Worse than these, however, was the petted, spoiled patient, who cried and pouted, and the one whose convalescent whims gave trouble.

The trained nurse must be a strong character, for her position is a trying one. Dixie had a charge that persisted in making love to her. He was slow in recovering from a serious operation, and he declared he did not want to get well enough to leave unless she would promise to leave with him. So fervent did he become that she persuaded the head nurse to allow her to exchange with another girl. The man was almost immediately well enough to be wheeled about the corridors, where he would lie in wait for her. He sent her flowers and presents, and wrote her love-letters. Her cold demeanor and polite replies that she could not return his affection, and her emphatic refusal of his offer of marriage, only made him the more ardent; but, when he was discharged as cured, she heard no more of him. Evidently, he had dropped back into an old groove of life—perchance returned to an old love, or, who knows, found a new.

During her second year, she found several patients who thought a nurse a piece of public property to be used or abused according to their fancy or whims. They paid for treatment and nursing, and, with the inconsistency of the near-sick, expected every caprice to be gratified, whether reasoable or not. They found one nurse, however, that fully understood her calling and had the qualities of tenderness and tact well balanced by will-power and courage. She did not undertake to lecture them, nor did she assume the air of injured innocence. Her attitude was that of assistant physician.

Her character and tact were quickly recognized and the superintendent told her she was destined to become a head nurse if she wished such a position. Her plans, however, were more in keeping with her father's ambition. She was only too anxious for her apprenticeship to come to an end, so she could join forces with her parents in the fight against the Monster. She told a few of the other nurses about the things her father had discovered, and the warfare he had taken up against social sin, and the little company began to study the question together. They were alarmed at the number of patients who were in the House of Healing on account of this very thing, and, from doctors, women, and older nurses, they gathered facts that made them thankful Jim Miller had arisen to lead the great campaign. Dixie obtained promises from a goodly number of these nurses to help her in the school she was to head, and of others to become lecturers in the public schools when laws were passed to that effect.

The Man learned of her father and his sorrows, and of the revenge he had undertaken; also of the part Dixie was to play in it all; and he sent for her and gave her his benedicton.

"You will meet much opposition, Miss Miller; those who lead reforms always do. Your father has found that out. You must make up your mind to spend your life without seeing very much accomplished; but you are engaging in a righteous cause, and the work you begin will be taken up by those who come after you, and generations will rise up and call you blessed. Tell your father that my poor work is only to repair the damage after it is done; but his mighty task is to prevent the wrecks. That is far the greater work."

"I thank you for these noble, cheering words. If we may have the approval of such men as you, we will not care for the opposition, nor for the time it takes to firmly establish the work. But, to compare what we are hoping to do with the magnificent thing you have already accomplished seems like sacrilege. Your work is akin to that of the Christ."

"Ah, but it is so limited! We help a few

thousands—your father is helping the whole race. Thank God that you may help him in his God-given work."

It was always thus. The Man had the wonderful gift of inspiring others to great deeds, and never put himself, nor the institution he had brought into being, forward as an example. Dixie went from his presence strangely exhilarated and confident.

She wrote her father about this conversation, and was delighted when he replied that the encouragement had come when he needed it most. His enemies were doing their utmost to prevent his return to the senate, and this timely word gave him inspiration to throw himself into the struggle with new vigor.

Drury had finished his service in the House of Healing, and had returned to Tamalpias to carry out his contract with Dr. McConnell. She wrote him, also, of the talk with the Man, and it warmed his heart and made him resolve to do his best for the suffering ones about him. He wondered if the Man knew how his words were repeated and passed on to the teeming thousands, giving cheer, firing ambition, warming selfish hearts, and stirring enthusiasm. Again, he determined to be like him. His reply to Dixie's letter recorded the renewal of that resolution, and her heart was glad. She longed for the right and the opportunity to help him achieve such character and greatness.

CHAPTER XVII.

DRURY PATTERSON, M. D.

It would have been difficult for Drury to nave returned to Tamalpias for the practise of his profession, had he not become the protege and partner of Dr. McConnell. His life and character were so clean that he had no fears along that line; but the old proverb is true: "A prophet is not without honor save in his own country." He had arrived at Tamalpias when he was a mere boy, and he knew everybody. "Familiarity breeds contempt," and he was timid about claiming knowledge and ability in his profession among those who had never discovered anything unusual in his caliber or attainments. True, he had won honors in the high school; but some one did that every year. Beyond all this was the stern fact that he was the child of a drunkard who had died of delirium tremens. The townfolk did not hold this against him in any definite way; however, he knew that it would be used in case he aroused any opposition. He shrank from the possibility of such aspersion, yet he knew that his position on certain questions, and the things that would come up in the practice of his profession, would engender competitive opposition and criticism, and the enmity of those whose calls for illegal work he must preemptorily decline. Much of this would be avoided by entering the firm as junior partner. Dr. McConnell would become fully responsible for everything that came up in the practice, and Drury would have his advice and counsel. The old Doctor treated him more as a son than as a partner, and Drury looked on him as a father. Their talks were frank and full of mutual confidence, and the older man fully recognized the up-to-date training and education of the younger.

It was a brisk fall morning, and the young Doctor was invigorated by his morning bath and the long walk in the fresh air, when he came down the street to the office. As he neared the stairway, he noticed a new sign swinging at the entrance. His pulse quickened and his breast heaved with pride as he read the gilt letters:

"DRS. McCONNELL & PATTERSON,
Physicians and Surgeons."

He did not know the order for the sign had been given, and his surprise was complete. An old schoolmate was passing and stopped to congratulate him, and his cup was full to overflowing. He had dreamed of the time when his name would be announced as a healer of men; but to have it coupled like this, with the name of such a successful doctor as this dear old man who had made a place for himself in every heart and home in the Valley, was more than he had expected for ten years to come. His experience in the House of Healing had given him ease and grace in the sick-room, as well as ability to inspire the confidence of family and patient. His first calls were made in the company of Dr. McConnell; but it was not long until it became necessary for him to visit some of their patients by himself.

His only embarrassment was when he was called to see old playmates or schoolmates. He soon saw, however, that their embarrassment was greater than his, and that helped him to gain that poise and equilibrium that quickly overcame all timidity and sensitiveness. Indeed, it was not long until he was called, by preference, to many homes where his partner had attended for years. His bright disposition, which had been a striking characteristic since childhood, was a valuable asset in any sick-room. His touch was light and his manner gentle; his methods were firmness and promptitude; his demands were cleanliness and cheerfulness, and he never talked of himself nor paraded his knowledge.

Under his treatment and suggestion, several chronic cases that had been under treatment for years were cured, and these persons went about singing his praises. He was reputed to have cured young Martin Williams of a malady that had baffled many doctors; but he and Martin knew that his medicine had been compounded mostly of sound lecturing and helpful advice.

Marvin Harris had married Thelma Dawson, and they spent the summer in Michigan. When they came home in October, Marvin scoffed at the idea of Drury Patterson being in the active practice of medicine, and especially, being a partner of Dr. McConnell.

"What is the matter with Dr. McConnell, anyhow? he ought to have better sense than to take that fellow in with him. What can he ever amount to? Why, it means the death of the folks that have him. Of course, these young doctors must have somebody to experiment on; but Drury Patterson will kill more people than he will ever cure." He talked like that until Dr. McConnell heard it, and went to him. Even then, he refused to believe that the son of a drunkard like John Patterson could ever amount to anything. There were a few who sided with him, and they told Dr. McConnell that he must never send Drury to see their sick.

An epidemic of scarlet fever broke out in December, and the schools were closed on account of it. Drury threw himself into the work of checking the disease with such vigor that all the doctors were astounded. His methods were new to them, and the response to his use of the serum was so prompt and effective that he was called in consulation with every doctor in the Valley. If anything was needed to establish him firmly after that, it came when three cases of diphtheria almost threw the town into panic, and he was successful in the use of that serum. Marvin Harris' baby was two weeks old when Dr. McConnell was stricken with a fever. He sent Drury to make a call there in his stead; but Marvin would not receive him. Although the insult was keen, Drury was more concerned about the afflicted baby than he was about the unjust words of his old rival. At that particular time, the only other doctor to be had was a man who was somewhat dissipated, and who had very little practice. He was called, and told them there was nothing wrong with the child's eyes except that he had taken a little cold, which had settled in them. Mrs. Harris was not doing well, and they sent for a trained nurse, when who should be detailed for this service but Dixie Miller! She was glad to undertake the duty, as it would take her home for a short time. She did not know whom she was to serve until she arrived, nor did they know who would be sent. Marvin and Thelma were both delighted when Dixie arrived, and she was soon installed in charge of both mother and child. It took her only a few hours to become convinced that there was more than "cold" wrong with the baby's eyes, and she asked the privilege of carrying it to Dr. McConnell's home, that he might see it. This was done, and the old physician sent for Drury immediately. To the experienced young doctor, there was hardly need of miscroscopic examination before pronouncing the trouble ophthalmia. He had learned to be painstaking, however, and he did not give his diagnosis until he had the evidence of science. Since Dr. Patterson had been insulted and forbidden the home of Marvin Harris, and since Dr. McConnell was too ill to treat the child, the only thing to be done was to send for the father and talk with him. This Dr. McConnell did. When he came, the Doctor said:

"Marvin, I am a sick man, and do not know that I shall ever get well. If I was able, I would undertake to treat your baby's eyes. You have refused the services of Dr. Patterson for no other reason than your prejudice, and foolish enmity. I can not say anything about the doctor you have employed, but I am compelled to tell you that, under the present treatment, or lack of it, your child will be blind within a month. Your wife is not able to take it away for treatment, nor is that necessary; Dr. Patterson can cure it as well as any specialist in the world. Lay aside your prejudice and let him serve your child."

"What is the trouble with the baby's eyes, Dr. McConnell?"

"Ophthalmia."

"What is that?"

"It is the same disease that destroyed Little Jim Miller's eyes."

"What! Is that what Jim Miller is lecturing about?"

"Exactly."

"But I never——"

"Hold on, Marvin. Remember you are talking to your own physician now. You might plead innocence to another, but not to me. You laughed at me when I told you the truth. Now, your child is suffering for your sin, and this trouble must be attended to at once if you would save the sight of the babe."

"Are you sure of this, Doctor?"

"Absolutely. I had Dr. Patterson examine a specimen from the baby's eyes under the microscope, and there can be no doubt about it."

"And Dixie Miller and Drury Patterson know all about this?"

"Yes. Miss Miller knew it at once. That is why she brought the child to me."

"My God! I would rather any one in the world would know it than they, except my father and my wife. Must they know it?"

"No need for that. Dr. Patterson will never tell a soul what the trouble is, nor will Miss Miller. They are trained to keep professional secrets. The treatment will not arouse suspicion, and the child will be well in a short time."

"My wife will not know?"

"Not through doctor or nurse."

"Well, I suppose there is nothing else to be done. Send Drury right away, if he will come."

"No. I want you to be a man. You insulted him; now go to the office and apologize to him, then ask him to take the case. He is a perfect gentleman, and he would attend the child if I asked him to. You owe it to him, though, and to yourself, to go to him like a man and ask him to take the case."

"You are asking me to do a hard thing."

"No, sir, I am asking you to do a big thing, a manly thing. If you are a real gentleman, you will do it."

"All right, Doctor, I will do it."

He found Dr. Patterson busy and had to wait for his turn to be admitted to the consultation-room. While he waited, he looked about. There, on the wall, beside Dr. McConnell's ancient sheepskin, was Drury Patterson's diploma, and his license from the State Medical Board. It began to dawn on him that he had turned a man from his door who was fully recognized by the highest authority in his profession, and all for puerile reasons, too. Some of the waiting patients were discussing the Doctor, and they all, with one accord, declared him a wonderful healer. Their very presence there was proof of their faith in his powers, and Marvin began to wish for his turn to come to enter that mysterious room where secrets are carried in, but never carried out. At last, Dr. Patterson came out with an old man, and, when he had dismissed him, turned and extended his hand to Marvin.

"How are you, Mr. Harris?" he said, with the utmost earnestness. "What can I do for you?"

"I want to consult you privately, Dru——Dr. Patterson."

"Step into my room."

Marvin found it difficult to come to the matter in hand. He felt, as never before, that he was the vagabond, the outcast. He knew that Drury had always shunned the very sin that was now proving his own ruin. He had called him the child of a drunkard, while he himself had been worse than a drunkard. Dr. Patterson saw his confusion and asked:

"How is Mrs. Harris?"

"She is not getting well at all. There is no use in beating about the bush, Doctor. You know my awful fix and what brings me here. I was a cad to treat you as I did. You always beat me at athletics; you excelled me in school; you won the lasting love of the girl I wanted to marry; and I allowed my foolish prejudice and jealousy to overbalance my judgment. I ask you to pardon my nasty words, and forget that I ever acted so rudely to you."

"You embarrass me, Marvin. I assure you that I have no ill-will toward you, and shall never think of all that again."

"Thank you, Doctor. With your pardon, I also ask your service in saving the eyes of my child, if it is not too late. Dr. McConnell told me plainly what the disease is, and I am sure you can not have the respect for me that I have for you. You have always been so clean and pure; that is one reason I have not been courteous to you; but I have more respect for you, now that I realize what I have done."

"That is noble. We will not discuss it any further, just now. I will be out to see the baby within an hour. God bless you and help us to save the little eyes."

Marvin's hardest task was to enter the presence of the nurse who knew him so well, and who now knew him for what he really was. Never had his proud spirit been so humbled, and he thought he could see why Maury Tallman had taken his own life. That was what he would do if his baby's eyes were not saved. And to think that this young doctor and this nurse, should be the ones to discover the trouble and provide the cure, was almost more than he could bear.

Dixie was as kind and unembarrassed as if she was in the home of her own kindred, and she seemed to love the baby from the very first. Mrs. Harris was overjoyed at the attention and capability of the nurse, and told Marvin she was a perfect angel.

Dr. Patterson soon had the case well in hand and was gratified to see the steady improvement in the eyes. The other doctor had been dismissed before he took charge of the case, and Drury was also asked to attend the mother. He found her suffering intensely, and soon decided that she would have to undergo an operation. This was such a shock to Marvin that he became desperate, and it was with difficulty that Dr. Patterson dissuaded him from his purpose to follow Maury Tallman in taking his own life. To make matters worse, in a fit of remorse, he went into the invalid's room and told her the whole horrid story, and explained to her the cause of the baby's narrow escape and her own infirmity. The shock was very great, but no greater than the effect on her attitude to him. She spurned him, and threatened to leave him and secure a divorce. He begged and sobbed, but she was obdurate. In his distress he turned to Dixie and implored her to intercede for him. It is well she had such marvelous tact and powers of persuasion, for it was the hardest task she ever undertook. For more than a week, she argued, and urged his ignorance and his repentance. Dr. Patterson added his plea to Dixie's but, it was not until they told her that Marvin was breaking down, and would likely destroy himself, that she relented and sent for him; and, just like a woman, her forgiveness was full and complete, and the fire only welded their love more firmly than it had ever been.

There was no one prouder than Dr. McConnell when Dixie took the baby over to let him see it after it was well. Its bright eyes sparkled in their clearness, and it responded to his play with smiles and baby laughter.

"It is a happy day for me," he told Dixie. "I have loved Drury Patterson ever since I first saw him. I knew he would make his mark, and I am doubly pleased that he has chosen my profession. Why, the saving of these little eyes is a greater blessing than some people have ever been to the world."

"I am glad you have been such a friend to him, Dr. McConnell. You have helped and inspired him more than you know."

"I suspect you have been more inspiration to him than any one else. Of course, you understand that I know why you have not married, Dixie. There never was a nobler, cleaner man than Dr. Patterson; he is as fine and pure as he can be, and I sincerely wish he did not have John Patterson's blood in his veins. You are both the most sensible young people I ever knew."

"Thank you for your kind words, Doctor. We are both happy in the work we have chosen, and the privilege of co-operating in this one case is a measure of compensation."

Marvin Harris, watching them in their work, envied them. They were more like two doctors working in perfect harmony than two lovers, for they never allowed themselves to become silly. Their love was too sacred to talk much about. It was only when they congratulated themselves on the success of their efforts, as they held hands for a moment and looked into each other's eyes with pride, that the fires burned on the altars of their hearts with more than usual fervor. It was an undying affection that was made holy by the barriers to its consummation. He had wonderful control of himself, for he knew that the battle was mostly his. The maternal instinct was very strong in Dixie. She dreamed of nursing the Harris baby, and, several times, the dreams transformed her into a modern madonna. She would awaken with a strange feeling that the baby on her arm was her own; then, her sorrow would amount almost to rebellion at the circumstances that forbade her the exalted privilege of motherhood.

When Mrs. Harris was able, Dr. Patterson took her to the city, that she might have the advantage of the equipment of the House of Healing and the services of the best surgeons in the State. Dixie returned with him, and was made special nurse in the case. The operation was successful, and the surgeon said she would entirely recover if complications did not arise. Marvin was entirely subdued, and his friends knew he would never be the same impetuous man again. His parents never knew what the trouble was with either mother or baby, and his wife came to look on it all as an unavoidable thing over which neither of them had any control. She was content with her child, her husband, and her nice home, and did not propose to worry over the mistakes of the past nor the woes of others.

Drury was too busy to sit down and recount his successes; but he was happy in seeing suffering alleviated, and the gratitude of those he served fully repaid him for the harsh words of the few enemies who tried to disparage him. But his greatest joy was that he was pleasing his benefactor, Jim Miller. The Senator knew about the baby, and he told the young doctor how much he appreciated his ability to save eyes like that. He forbade the young doctor ever to offer to repay him the loan with which he had secured his education; he declared he wanted that much investment in the great work already done, and in what should yet be done. It was part of his revenge for the injuries to his own loved ones.

Mrs. Miller and Jessie Tallman were also valuable friends of the junior member of the firm of McConnell and Patterson. They entertained him and recommended him to such purpose that he was called into the best homes in the Valley, and was soon established in the largest practice any one doctor had ever had. His fees were large because he was called to attend cases that were formerly sent away for expert treatment in the cities. Other doctors went about in their slow-going buggies; but he drove an automobile, and was at the bedside of a patient before the others could hitch up and start. When Dr. McConnell recovered from his illness he took care of the office practice, and turned over the visiting to Dr. Patterson.

CHAPTER XVIII.

A RAY OF LIGHT FOR DRURY.

Dr. Patterson purchased a neat modern cottage and installed his mother there. She never went out; indeed, she had never mingled in the social circles of Tamalpias. Since her widowhood, she had been more of a recluse than ever. Drury urged her to entertain friends, and to accept the invitations that came, for his sake; but she could not bring herself to undertake the responsibilities, and told him that she would be more apt to embarrass him than to help. He accepted the situation, while deploring it. His nature demanded social intercourse, and his profession made it almost imperative, if he was to be more than an ordinary country doctor. His mother's decision caused him to think, more than ever before, what a help Dixie Miller could be to him in making his life count. More than once he wondered why his nature was so different from his mother's, to say nothing of the wide dissimilarity between him and the elder Patterson.

Mrs. Patterson was very careful for his comfort, and always had his meals served to his exact taste and convenience. His clothes were always in the best of order, and he could count on her to see that the yard-man kept things according to his instructions. What she lacked in social qualities, she made up in housekeeping and home-making ability and management. She was a very devout woman. Many times, when he would come in late at night, he would find her reading her Bible or praying. She was a regular attendant at her church on Sunday mornings, and contributed liberally out of her allowance from Drury.

He studied her closely and came to the conclusion that something was preying on her mind. He resolved to ask her about it, and, one rainy night, when they were alone, he said to her:

"Mother, I am afraid there is something troubling you. Are you worrying over something?"

She was startled, and looked at him curiously for some time before replying. "What makes you think so, Drury?"

"Well, I have noticed you sitting in brown study so often, and your religious attitude gives one the impression that there is an old sore in your memory. I do not want to be inquisitive, but I thought it might be something that you could share with me. Perhaps I could help you."

"No, no. It is nothing. I am all right. Perhaps I am dwelling too much on the past, but—"

She stooped and sighed deeply. Then, she got up and kissed his forehead, and left the room without a word. The incident confirmed his conviction that there was a skeleton in the past of which he knew nothing, and his mother seemed to prefer that he should not know. He did not like the mystery. If there was anything that had taken place in the family to make her like that, he ought to know it, and he would; he would demand of her to tell him the first opportunity that presented itself.

The next morning she was indisposed, and he found she had a high fever. He prescribed for her and told her she would be all right in a few days. When she failed to improve according to expectations, he sent for Dixie Miller to come and nurse her. She steadily grew worse, and he called Dr. McConnell into consultation. Her symptoms indicated mental or nervous affection; but she refused to tell them whether there was anything on her mind. Drury made an attempt to secure her confidence in the matter, but she broke down and sobbed so that he abandoned the effort. He was sitting with her one day while Dixie was at dinner, when she cried softly for several minutes. He asked her what the matter was that grieved her so, and she reached for his hand and drew him down to her.

"O Drury," she said, "you will never know how I have loved you! I wish I could tell you my trouble, but I can not. I promised Mr. Patterson I would never tell a living soul, and I must keep my vow. It almost drives me crazy at times. Promise me that you will always love me."

"Why, Mother, dear, of course I will always love you. I fear you are not yourself today. Try to rest and get well; then, we will talk it over, and you must tell me what it is. If it concerns me, I ought to know it."

"Yes, it concerns you. Let me see. Where was I? It was terrible, wasn't it? And I caught hold of the rope, and just then you leaped into my arms, and I—Drury, where are you?"

"Here I am, Mother, darling. What is it you are trying to tell me?"

"Tell you? I was not trying to tell you anything. What did I say?"

Then, it dawned on him that she was delirious, and the awful thought that her mind was almost shattered struck him dumb.

"What was I saying, Drury?"

"Nothing, dear. You were just tired. Do you want to go to sleep? There now. Just go to sleep."

Dixie came to relieve him, and he turned sadly from the room and went to his office. Then, the duties of the afternoon claimed his attention, and he almost forgot the thousand surmises the few words she had spoken in her delirium had sent through his mind.

Soon after he left, Mrs. Patterson aroused from a stupor into which she had sunk, and looked earnestly at Dixie for some time. Then she spoke quietly.

"Why haven't you and Dr. Patterson married?"

The question was so simple, and asked in such an innocent way, that Dixie was shocked. Yet she could not turn the suffering woman aside with an evasive answer.

"Do you not know?"

"No. I have often wondered, and thought I would ask Drury some time."

"Well, we believe it would be unsafe for us to marry under the circumstances."

"O I remember. He said something like that to me the day Mr. Patterson died. He seemed to be afraid that he, he—What do I want to say? Afraid he—O yes, afraid he would some day be a drunkard. No. not just that. But he won't, and I know why; but I must not tell. John Patterson said he would kill me if I told. I won't tell. I won't tell."

"No, you must not tell, unless you want to tell just me. Do you want to tell me?"

"I wish I could tell you. You have been so good to me, and you are going to marry Drury. Drury and his wife ought to know. But that would be giving the whole thing away, and it was wrong. I couldn't help it, could I? He made me do it. Then, I got to loving the baby as well as if he was my own. and I did not want to give him up. He was so sweet, and he was just the same age as my baby, too. No, I won't tell. I musn't."

"That is right; you musn't tell anybody but me," Dixie managed to say.

She was breathing hard, for she could gather from what the semi-delirious woman had already said that there was some mystery about to be unfolded. Instinctively, she knew, also that it concerned the parentage of the man she loved. Her wits were active and she determined to use them to get at the truth this woman knew; for, if she did not learn the facts now. they might never be known.

"And your baby died, did it?" she asked.

"Died? No, my baby was drowned. Didn't you see it float down in the muddy water. I tried to get it, but they wouldn't let me. And the fire was so hot it blistered my face. Then I caught hold of the rope, and there he came into my arms just as if the angels put him there. His trunk was carried ashore, too. Weren't the little dresses pretty? And that one with the hand-embroidery was the one I had been watching all the way up the river, and wishing I had it for my baby. She was such a grand lady."

Suddenly she broke off and began sobbing, and talking incoherently. Dixie tried to soothe her, and get her to tell her more. She called for Dr. Patterson over the telephone; but he had gone on a long trip to consult with another doctor; so she renewed her efforts to get the whole story from Mrs. Patterson. The fever was very high and the patient was worse than she had ever been. Dixie bathed her until the fever was cooled, and then encouraged her to talk about her baby.

"So you took the trunk, and Drury, and kept them instead of your baby, did you?"

"Who told you that? John Patterson would be mad if he knew some one had told that. But I didn't tell it, did I?"

"No, you did not tell it; I just know it. Where did you go then?"

"We went to New Orleans, and then to California; but she never did get my baby. Don't let them get my baby while I am gone."

"No, they shall not get your baby. You know

your baby was drowned, and you found Drury and took him to be your baby. Was his mother drowned?"

"Yes, I went to the funeral, to be sure. His father was there by the grave, and I was afraid of him; but John said he would not let him get the baby. Then, we ran away."

"And the boat burned while you were on it."

"No, it was not a boat. Let me see—all right, John, I won't tell him. Please don't. Oh, save me! save me!"

Thus, bit by bit, the faithful nurse got the story as far as the failing mind of the invalid could tell it. Her lapses of memory became more frequent, and her delirium soon became hysteria; that, in its turn, quickly developed mania. About five o'clock, she tried to sit up in the bed, and cried and talked incoherently. Finally she pointed at an old desk she had clung to through the years, and cried:

"Bring me that paper."

"What paper?" asked Dixie.

"Long paper . . . drawer."

She fell back on the pillows in a stupor, and Dixie was still working to restore her when Drury came in. She sank rapidly, and never regained consciousness. She murmured an occasional word, but they could not catch what she was saying.

Friends came in to watch with them, and Dixie could not bring herself to tell Drury of the story she had gathered while the woman who had been a mother to him lay dying like that. It seemed to him that everything he had to cling to was leaving him. He loved Dixie Miller, but he could never marry her. He loved his profession, but he would never have a home again, and his home had meant so much to him. Mrs. Patterson had cared for him and been tender to him, even though she had not been a helpful companion during his years of study.

Dixie stole up-stairs and sat down in her room to think it all out. If the story she had gathered in fragments from the dying woman was true, Drury Patterson was not the child of a drunkard. The nervous strain had been almost too much for her, and she threw herself on the bed and cried. It was almost too good to be true. Then, she thought of the paper Mrs. Patterson had called for. However, it would be time enough to look for that after she had told Dr. Patterson what she had learned.

Lower and lower ebbed the tide of life in the body of the woman who had given to Drury Patterson the best that was in her. She went quietly to sleep, and Drury could not help contrasting her death with that of her dissipated husband. It was Jim Miller who lifted him from beside the bed and led him out on the lawn, where he consoled him with kind words and manly sympathy.

"Mr. Miller," said the bereaved young man, "you have been more of a father to me than my own father was. He was kind in his way; but he never did give me his confidence, nor allowed me to give him mine. Mother was gentle and kind to me always. She told me, often, that she wanted me to be a fine gentleman—finer than any of the Pattersons. She has always acted very peculiarly about me, and, somehow, made me feel that there was a mystery in the family that I ought to know about. You are an old resident here, and you ought to know something about my family.

"But I do not, Drury. I knew your father before he went to Georgia to visit some of his relatives; but he did not return here until you were about twelve years old. During that interval, his parents died and left him the place where you were raised. I am sure your supposed mystery was only a fancy of your mother's."

"Perhaps you are right; I wish I knew."

Dr. McConnell was also a great mainstay to his young partner in this dark hour. He cheered him, and counseled him as a father. Mr. Harris, too, showed his sympathy and friendship by asking the privilege of taking charge of affairs until the funeral should be over. Drury accepted his kind offer, and never regretted it.

The funeral was beautiful and the concourse of people proved the popularity of the bereaved son. The floral offerings were many and unique. If such tokens can soften grief, Dr. Patterson had balm enough to cure his wounded spirit very soon. Marvin Harris sent the most expensive design, a Gothic harp with the word, "Mother," on the base. Dixie's offering was a simple little bouquet of lilies-of-the valley. Kind hands had covered John Patterson's grave with flowers, and Drury knew that his place in the hearts of the people was secure.

CHAPTER XIX.

"NOT UNTIL I FIND OUT."

It would have been a simple matter for Dixie Miller to have told Drury Patterson of her experience with Mrs. Patterson if she could have done so immediately. Circumstances prevented it, and the longer the task was delayed, the more difficult it became. She realized that it would not do to disturb his mind with it while she was alive, and, when the woman was dead, the nurse could not bring herself to unfold a problematic story that might intrude on the sacredness of the funeral. Then, too, this woman had been a mother to him; and he owed her all the respect he was showing, for his bereavement was as real as though she was his mother in fact.

The task grew more delicate with the lapse of time, and the events that were happening so rapidly. For several days after the funeral, Dr. Patterson was out of town by the advice of Dr. McConnell, and, when he returned, Dixie failed to get him over the telephone for some reason. At last, she wrote him a note, asking him to call to see her at his earliest convenience. He came to her father's home that night; but his conversation was about his mother, and it was evident he had placed her on a pedestal in his memory from which Dixie could scarcely bring herself to cast her. She was afraid, also, that he might think she had a selfish motive in trying to disprove his kinship to the Pattersons. Gradually, however, she turned the conversation to make her duty easier of performance.

"Did your mother ever hint at a burden on her mind that was crushing her and sapping her health, Drury?"

"Yes, Dixie, and I have wanted to ask you if she said anything to you during her illness that would throw light on her trouble?"

"She talked a great deal, that last afternoon, after you left. It was so incoherent, though, that I scarcely know what to make of it. I am going to ask you a serious question, Drury, and one that may shock you; but I feel it my duty to ask it frankly: did it ever occur to you, or have you ever had reason to doubt, that you were John Patterson's child? Wait, dear." She took his hand in both of hers. "You know how it frequently happens that a child dies in infancy, and the parents adopt a child to take its place."

"What do you mean, Dixie? Did she tell you that?"

"No, not just that. Please don't get excited. She did not really tell me anything; but she talked in her delirium, and, if what she said had any foundation in fact, I gathered that she and Mr. Patterson were on a boat with their baby; there must have been some kind of an accident, and her baby was drowned. She was rescued with you in her arms, and they kidnapped you, and raised you as their own baby. She said she saw the lady—your mother, I take it—buried, and your father was at the grave. Then, she and Mr. Patterson went to New Orleans, and finally, to California. Where were you when you can first remember?

"O, I do not know. I remember long trips on the cars, and one trip on a ship. It must have been Cuba that we visited when I was five or six years old. Then, we lived in Georgia when we got the message that the grandparents were dead; but there was no mystery in that, for it was the old home of the Pattersons. If I was not John Patterson's child, nobody there knew it, I am sure. Tell me all she said that day."

She told him all that had happened, and he told her of the remarks Mrs. Patterson had made to him the day Mr. Patterson died, and what she had said in her delirium before Dixie had entered the room.

"O, I had not thought of it before; but Father said something like that when he was dying. Let's see, what were his exact words? I have it! He said: 'I had to do it. All the devils were pulling at me, and one stuck out his tongue and cursed me. He made me do it. Go away, go away, and let me get on the boat. There he is! He is going to choke me. There they all come. Fire! Fire!' Before that, he yelled at me to go away, and said that I looked like 'he' did the night of the fire. They would not both talk of a 'boat,' and 'fire,' and act so strangely, without some experience that had impressed their subconscious minds, causing them to do it."

"I have not told you her last words, yet. She sat up in the bed and told me to bring her the paper. I asked her what paper, and she replied 'long paper.' Then, there were several mumbled words I could not understand. She pointed to the desk, and ended with the word, 'drawer'. I am sure there is a paper in that desk that will throw light on the subject."

Drury leaped to his feet and took her arm, pulling her up from her chair.

"Come, let us go to my cottage and hunt for that paper, right now."

"That would not do, Drury. Can't you see it would not do, tonight?"

"We will take your father along. Go ask him to come here."

She flew to the sitting-room, and soon had her father in the parlor, where they explained the whole matter to him as quickly as possible. Jim Miller was in the midst of his second campaign, and he was very tired; but he readily consented to go with them to investigate this new-found hope that would mean so much to his own child.

Dr. Patterson drove his machine furiously through the road leading to town, and they were soon in the room where Mrs. Patterson had died. The desk was an old-fashioned affair that she had told Drury was made by her father, who was a cabinet-maker. The key was in the lock, and Drury quickly opened the top, and the three drawers. There were many papers and letters in the dawers, and it took them a long time to go through them. None of them had anything to do with the matter in hand, unless it was an occasional reference in some letters from a correspondent who wrote a very good hand, and signed his name, "Basil." They gave up the search, and Drury was about to close the desk when he saw an envelope that had something in it. It was unsealed and plain. He took out the letter that was enclosed, and read it. It began, "Dear Brother," and referred to receiving his letter. Then, it went on: "I feel my strength leaving me, and sometimes my mind is all in a muddle. I am glad I told you about my trouble, for it seems that since John died I will go crazy thinking about it all. I am afraid I will die with this thing haunting me down to the grave. I wish I could tell Drury all about it, but I know he would hate me, and that would be the worst punishment that could come to me. Oh I just can't think of his ever knowing that he is not my child."

The letter fell from Drury's fingers, and he staggered back to a chair, and dropped into it.

"My God!" he cried, "Who am I? A nameless waif cast up by the muddy waters of the Mississippi. A man without a name. O, my good friend Miller, what shall I do? It was bad enough to be the child of a drunkard, but to be a nameless man; a thing of destiny, not knowing whence I came. I have wept over the graves of parents who were no parents. I loved them, and now I discover them to be criminals, selfish criminals, who robbed a drowned mother of her child, stole a babe away from its father, and bequeathed me nothing except the name of a drunkard, all to satisfy themselves, and substitute me for the babe they lost that terrible day or night."

Father and daughter tried to comfort him; but his grief must run its course. When Jim Miller made some suggestions about following up the slender clew that might lead to the discovery of his parentage, he waved it aside.

"Leave me here for the night, dear friend. I will come to you in the morning, if I may, and will ask you to help me to formulate some plans. For the present, I must think."

"Of course, you may come to me, and I will not spare time nor money to help you learn the truth. Your sun has not gone down, my boy. The morning will bring you clearer vision, and you may look back to this as the best day that has ever come into your life."

Dixie put her arms about his neck and gave him her lips.

"I believe in you, Drury, and, like Father, I am sure you will some day thank God for finding that letter. If it gives you the inheritance you have longed for, it will be worth while, won't it, dear?"

"Yes, yes, and that would mean that I could have you, Dixie! O God, grant that it may be so."

Jim Miller turned back to them and put his arms about them. His tears mingled with theirs, and, for some minutes, he stood with them thus.

"God bless you, my children. May your hopes be realized in the very near future. Be brave, my boy, and hope for the best until you know the facts." He kissed them both, and left them for a time.

Although the cup was bitter, there was so much sweetness mingled with it that Drury was glad that he had drunk it. Dixie Miller's love and confidence were worth all that he suffered, and her bright prophecies seemed so reasonable that he took courage, and made her many promises. Through the following year, this night was his guiding star, and the memory is sweet to him today.

At their conference the next morning, it was decided that Drury should go to Cromwell, Georgia, and try to locate Mrs. Patterson's brother, Basil. She had mentioned this brother to Drury, but he had never seen him. Indeed, he had never met any of her relatives. His plan was to visit the Pattersons and ask if they knew where he could find her relatives, and what their names were. He did not remember to have ever heard what her maiden name was. On one occasion, he had asked her, and she had told him that there were reasons why she preferred not to tell him about her people just then. She was always fond of telling incidents in her early home-life; but she never mentioned more than the given names of her one sister and one brother.

At Cromwell, Drury was received with joy. He found the Pattersons better people than he had expected, and they were well-to-do. It was hard for him to tell the leading man among them—a younger brother of John's—what his mission was. He told this man, Dick Patterson, the whole story, however, and showed him the letters he had brought with him.

"I am surprised beyond measure," said Mr. Patterson; "yet I am compelled to admit the conclusions to which you have come. Brother John married somewhere in Mississippi. We did not know his wife's people; but she was always a ladylike woman, and we accepted her without a question. Surely, she came of a good family. I heard, too, of the accident to the boat; but John would never talk about that more than to say that he and his wife got off with you before there was any danger. He was a very peculiar man, and none of us ever understood him. It would be just like him to do as you have reason to believe they did. I do not remember the name of the boat, nor where the accident took place; somewhere below Memphis, I think."

Drury returned to Memphis and went among the river-men, asking them about such an accident. They laughed at him when he could not give the name of the boat, nor the date of the supposed accident.

"Why, sir," said an old captain, "there have been so many accidents like that, you will have a hard time finding out about it unless you know the name of the boat, the date of the accident, or the place where it happened."

He saw how futile his search would be without more data than he had, and he was wasting time. He was sitting in the hotel reading the morning paper when his eye caught the advertisement of a detective agency. The very name, "detective," was repulsive to him; but he needed some one to work out his problems who was expert in such matters, and he decided to call up the manager and have him come to the hotel for an interview. This he did, and was so impressed with the man, and his dignity and quiet manners, that he employed him then and there to locate the man, Basil, and to get all the evidence possible in regard to such a steamboat accident as must have taken place twenty-five years before.

Jim Miller's disappointment was keen when Drury returned to Tamalpias with such meager results. He assured the young man, however, that he acted wisely in employing competent men to take up the quest. Not a word of all that had transpired was known to any one in the town except the Millers and Dr. McConnell. So Dr. Patterson took up his work as though nothing had happened. He and Dixie spent much time in each other's company, and she so inspired and cheered him that he worked harder and more effectively than he had ever done before. There was a change taking place in her that she discovered before he did, and she fought against it, too. She was rebellious over the fate circumstances had consigned them to, and her rebellion reached the point of expression one cool evening as they were driving down the river road.

"Drury, it was my father and I that decided that we must never marry," she said, "but, now that we know you are not the child of John Patterson, why should we have to know just whose child you are, before we do marry? We will likely never know, and I think it is foolish to deny ourselves the happiness in store for us just because you are the victim of an accident and a crime that deprives you of the name of your real parents."

"You make it hard for me, Dixie. I am trying to fight the battle like a real man, and I want you to help me."

"But isn't it an imaginary battle?"

"It may prove to be such; but for the present, it is real—only God knows how real."

"It is cruel! No other man and woman in the world were ever called on to sacrifice so much for so little. What do I care about the name you are known by? You are as clean and good as any man who walks the earth today, and better than hundreds who can trace their ancestry through countless generations. I love you, and I will marry you tomorrow and take the consequences."

"Is that in accordance with the promise you made to your father?"

Her face went white as she recalled that promise, but she rallied in a moment.

"That promise was made under the impression that you were certainly the child of a drunkard. Let me ask you, Drury: if it was to develop that I am not the daughter of Senator Miller, would you marry me, granted that your lineage was all right?"

"That is an unfair question, Dixie. Women are so much purer than men."

"Not by inheritance. If my father was a profligate, my child would inherit his appetites and passions as easily through me as my brother's child would through him."

"You have the best of that argument. But listen, sweetheart, how are we to know but that I have inherited worse than alcoholism from my parents? Oh, how gladly I would lead you to the altar tomorrow if I dared; but I can not, I can not. I would not present to your father a deformed child, nor cause another of his daughters to go to the operating table——Why, I would rather die tonight than to run the risk. No, Dixie, I love you too dearly to run the slightest risk of destroying your health, or bring sadness into your life, by accepting what would be the greatest joy that any man ever experienced at a matrimonial altar. We have been true to our ideals for a few years, let us go on until Heaven smiles upon us, and gives us the right to marry according to the teaching we have both received and know to be correct."

"Forgive me, darling, for my rashness. I am fully recovered, and see that you are right. That is the reason I love you so. You are the grandest and best man that lives. I am a better woman for this hour with you. You are strong; so strong, and I have derived strength from you."

"May I tell you now, dear, that you have endeared yourself to me more today than ever before?"

"I cannot see how."

"By revealing your feminine nature. I was beginning to think that you were almost too practical in regard to our affairs. Sometimes, I have looked on you as a sort of angel, too good to feel as deeply as a normal woman; at other times, you have seemed as practical as a doctor needs be. It is I who must ask forgiveness.'

"How noble you are! I am glad to be conquered like this by the man I love. If I revealed feminine nature, you have shown that, with all your gentleness you are a man. And I can pay you no higher compliment than to say that you are on even a higher pinnacle than the Man at the House of Healing. I have prayed that you might be like him, and now you are, and more than he is; for who knows what he would do under such circumstances as you have had to face?"

"There, girlie, you will turn my head pretty soon, so I suspect we had better drive back out of our paradise. We understand each other now, and we shall give ourselves to our work with renewed vigor. Perhaps it will not be long until the clouds clear away, and we shall appreciate the sunshine the more that we have been in the gloom."

The detectives reported locating the family of Mrs. Patterson. They were a fine family of Mississippi people; but they knew nothing of the exchange of babies. Basil Warren had died recently, and the others had not been in the confidence of Ellen, as they called Mrs. Patterson. From these relatives, however, the detectives had learned the date of her marriage to John Patterson, and the date of the birth of their baby. By this, they had figured the time of the supposed accident, and had located three different incidents, either of which might have been the one referred to. One had been an excursion boat, and the passengers had been required to register. In the other two cases, the registers had been lost. They were still at work on the case, and hoped to find out more that would be of value to the young physician.

Dr. Patterson locked up his cottage and took rooms at the Don Pedro hotel. He could not keep satisfactory servants, and he did not want to rent the cottage out; so he had the place cared for by his negro yard-man. It was frequently rumored that he and Dixie Miller were married on certain occasions; but the cottage remained closed, and Dixie went back to the House of Healing.

CHAPTER XX.

THE SECOND CAMPAIGN.

While the events recorded in the preceding chapters were happening. Jim Miller had been pushing the matters pertaining to his revenge. His first term in the State Senate did little more than to give him the opportunity to get a standing in politics, and to learn the rules of the game. He was astonished to find that everything was done *sub rosa.* Many of his colleagues made speeches on the floor of the Senate for the benefit of the galleries, and to be recorded in the proceedings and the daily press, then, privately agreed to the passage of the very bills they had spoken against.

Before his first session was nearly finished, Senator Miller decided that he must become a prominent figure in the politics of the whole State if he was to achieve anything worth while in the way of his great purpose. After a close study of the situation, and of the tactics of the leaders, he decided on a policy of publicity and frankness with the public through the press. He knew this would mean a fight with the "ring" from the Governor down; but he was willing to risk everything for the cause he was espousing, and he had the pleasure of knowing also that, if he did not win his personal battle, he would be giving the public an education that would be worth almost as much as the passage of the laws he was advocating. The more he pondered it, the more settled he became in the conviction that Maury Tallman had proposed the best remedy —education through the public schools.

Seeing the announcement of the annual meeting of the "Mothers' Congress," he attended its sessions, and was delighted to know that the public conscience was being aroused. He was invited to speak on the question of Social Purity, and the great throng of mothers and educators gave him such applause that he grew more eloquent than he ever thought he could be. When his address was finished, they gave him an ovation that meant more than he then knew. Thereafter, he was called on for addresses before the Child Welfare League of America, The National Health Society, The Purity League and the Women's Christian Temperance Union. He was in such demand for this kind of work that he feared his political fences would suffer decay. He was recompensed, however, by contact with great men and women who were in the fight with him, and he had access to a store of knowledge and facts that would be valuable when he returned to the fight in the Senate.

Jack Miller had returned from college and was ready to take up some kind of work. He was immediately attracted to the thing his father was doing, and attended several of the conventions and meetings his father addressed on the subject of the Great Black Plague of America. He wanted to take part in the fight in some way.

"All right, son," Senator Miller said, "I need

a secretary, and I shall be glad to have you serve me in that capacity."

"But Father, I shall want to make some speeches on this question myself. I am just boiling over to speak right now. Self-praise is half-scandal; but I was considered quite a speaker in college, and I won three medals in oratory. I surely ought to be able to speak on such an inspiring subject as this."

"Son, you do not know how you rejoice my heart. I have wondered who would take up the fight if I had to drop out before it is won. Speak! Yes, you shall speak as much as you wish, I will make engagements for you."

"I am glad you trust me, Father, and I promise you I will fight the battle until it is won or I die."

Senator Miller's cup was full as he told his wife of this interview. He felt the tingle of victory in his veins. He had lost a daughter and a son-in-law to the Monster; but he now had a son and daughter enlisted in his fight for revenge, and his wife and Jessie were helpers, also. Victory seemed so much nearer than ever before, and the wine in his cup was sweet.

There had been a spirit of rivalry between Tamalpias and Kimberly ever since the former had secured the railroad. Later, the county-seat had been removed to Tamalpias, and later still, saloons had been voted out of the beautiful valley town. This state of affairs caused the natural drifting of the better class of people to Tamalpias, and of the drinking, rowdy element to Kimberly. Bill Colton moved to Kimberly soon after his defeat by Jim Miller. He knew that he was out of the running for all time; but he hoped to be recognized as the Boss of the district, and that he could name the man who should make the second race against Senator Miller. In this, he was encouraged by the same source of supplies that had furnished the sinews of war in the first campaign. By handing out a little money here and there, he managed to recruit his forces, and, by treating to drinks and making barroom talks, he worked up much sentiment against Jim Miller. When the time seemed propitious, he began to mention an ex-judge of an adjoining county as the only man who could beat the man who was trying to take away their "personal liberty." None of the gangsters knew that he had been directed by the "bureau" that was furnishing him money to see to it that Judge Barr was nominated and elected. They did not care who was elected, so their enemy was defeated.

Thus it came to pass that the rivalry of towns and counties was introduced in order to befog the situation and divert the people from the real issue. Jim Miller knew that prejudice and sectional factions are hard to overcome, and he made speeches in which he tried to convince his hearers that his fight was not for any town or country, but for all humanity. It remained for Jack Miller, however, to plan the organization of parents and teachers into clubs for the study of social and educational problems. At first, the men would have little to do with the clubs; but, when their wives began to tell them of the papers that were being read, and the books that were being reviewed at the meetings, they became interested. Within thirty days, the whole district was aflame with the discussion of the very problems Jim Miller proposed to solve by the passage of certain laws. Once they got a glimpse of the real facts, these clubs called for more literature on the subject, and Jack saw that the right kind of books and periodicals were placed into the hands of the secretaries. So well and so quietly was the work performed that Bill Colton's crowd did not understand what was going on until the whole district was turning to Senator Miller as the only logical candidate to succeed himself. He was posted on the question, and his ability had been recognized by every national organization whose purpose was the uplift of the race.

Even the Senator, himself, did not recognize the master-stroke Jack had made until the sentiment had reached the stage that made his election by an overwhelming majority a foregone conclusion. Others recognized it before he did, and, less than a month before the primary election, a committee waited on Jack and asked him to become a candidate for the House of Representatives. The proposition was so sudden, and of such import, that he was confused for a little time. He asked for a day in which to consider it, and his request was granted. His father suggested his youth; but they remembered that there were two members of the previous legislature who were younger. It was finally decided that he would offer for the place, and the campaign began at once. Not a new campaign, but an intensified interest in the same one.

"Too much Miller," cried the opposition, "Why, they will be wanting to send their women to the Capitol next. We must not allow the whole family to be in the same legislature. Let the boy wait till the old man gets done running."

The people answered that this was a race for principles, not for men; these two men represented principles, and they were able to defend those principles. What matter that they were father and son? No others in the district and county were candidates on this platform, and the people proposed to give them a chance to pass the laws they were advocating. No greater victory was ever won for suffering women and children than that which Jim Miller and his noble son, Jack, won over the forces backed by the doctrine of "personal liberty." As before, nomination meant election, and both men began to get ready for the fight that would take place in the State Capitol the following winter.

For their better equipment and information, an organization of a local club was effected. Its membership was carefully selected from among the most influential and intelligent citizens. The superintendent of the city schools, Mr. Thompson, was chosen president, and the pastor of one of the churches was made secretary. The meetings were held weekly in the parlors of the San Pedro hotel. Dr. McConnell, Mr. Harris, Marvin Harris, Dr. Patterson, and a number of others united in the work. The secretary ordered circulars, booklets, and tracts from the different societies and Boards of Health, and the members were assigned subjects to write or speak on. The mistakes in solving the question were carefully noted, and the doubts of authorities in regard to this place and that were analyzed.

The gravest doubts expressed by students and doctors concerned Jim Miller's proposition that every applicant for license to wed should procure a certificate from two physicians attesting to his physical fitness to marry. The reasons put forward were carefully weighed, and debated at length. It was held by some that great progress had been made in the fight against tuberculosis by publicity concerning the disease, and that education was all that was needed. Jim replied that his proposed law was intended to afford relief until the masses could be educated.

It was Mr. Thompson who brought forward the idea of making a course in sanitary and moral prophylaxis, and the hygiene of sex, required by law in the State Normal schools, and that no certificates be granted to teachers who did not obtain full credits in such courses. This proposition was hailed with delight by the club as being the best suggestion yet made. Jack Miller told them of the address delivered to the students of the University of Pennsylvania at the beginning of each collegiate year by the physician in charge, and that many educational institutions were giving lectures and short courses along these lines on their own motion.

Many other measures were brought to the attention of the club and discussed with profit. Mr. Thompson suggested that the organization be made permanent, and that they open it to membership by application, admitting both sexes and widening the scope of its investigations and discussions to all questions of public health and moral. This was adopted, and a committee was appointed to work out the details and submit a constitution and by-laws, it being thoroughly understood that the club could not be used to further the personal interest of any person in a political way.

Dixie Miller came home in time to become an active member of the Tamalpias Health Club, and she was a valuable addition. Her presence removed the timidity of some who had hesitated to join, and it was only a short time until the membership numbered fifty. Dr. Patterson was sent East to attend several National societies, and to make further personal investigations of these important subjects. He was glad to go, as he was anxious to go deeper into the doctrine of heredity, and this would give him the opportunity to interview Dr. Grady, the great alienist.

The work of the campaign and the discussions in the Club had ripened Jack Miller into a fluent speaker, who had the vigor of youth, coupled with an exact knowledge of the matters he wanted to bring before the law-making body of his State. With the father working in the Senate and the scn in the House, their bills uniform, and acting in unison, they would have a mighty advantage over their opponents. Both men could scarcely wait for the convening of the legislature, so anxious were they to get into the fray.

The secretary of the Club had his eyes opened to the true state of affairs so thoroughly that he resigned his charge and went out to lecture over the State. He was surprised at the demand for such lectures. Ministers were awakening to the alarming situation, and churches were opened to him everywhere. He made a series of three addresses in each place; one to men on the subject, "The Dignity of Manhood," and to women on "True Womanhood," and one to young people on "Adolescence." Hundreds sought private interviews with him, and other hundreds told him, with tears running down their cheeks, that they wished they might have heard his addresses a few years earlier.

Jim Miller watched the minister's great work with a glowing heart. He was enjoying his revenge already. He even came to think, sometimes, that perhaps the Providence that had allowed the Monster to attack his home was a blessing in disguise. If the death and blindness of one or two could save the thousands, ought he not bow in thanksgiving to God that he was allowed to furnish the sacrifice for the altar of human emancipation? He felt that he could better understand the doctrine of the vicarious atonement, and he was resigned to the loss of his daughter as he never had been before. His wife fully shared this feeling, and Jessie found herself resigned to her loss in the same way. Indeed, Mrs. Tallman made liberal gifts to assist the minister to stay on the field, and was pleased when he told her that she would share in the reward that was to come as a result of the addresses.

That man is the greatest success who can get the most people to work for him. Some men fail because they try to do everything themselves. Others have the faculty of inspiring other workers and enlisting agencies that make their efforts successful. Jim Miller had the ability thus to grip men and things to the furtherance of his plans. Once he got the attention of an intelligent man, he was sure of that man's help; and there was no middle ground. He made that very plain. Every man was on one side or the other; to remain quiet was to assist the Monster in his work of destruction. If other men had built up a machine to advance their personal ambitions and interests, he gathered a host of men and women who hailed him as their leader in the greatest fight ever made in America for the crushing of a foe that had touched every one of their homes and lives in some way or another. If his son-in-law had felt like a Judas on the night of his self-destruction, Senator Miller felt like that patriot, Patrick Henry, must have felt when he uttered his immortal words: "Give me liberty, or give me death!" And he was now at a point where he could see emancipation of womankind written large on the horizon of the future. Soon, the fetters should fall off the limbs of more than half of the race, bound for thousands of years by the shackles of lust and ignorance.

His wife watched his transformation from the quiet stockman to the eloquent avenger and publicist with increasing amazement. All his latent forces and dormant energies were on fire. Nor did his zeal produce fanaticism. That was the best of it; he fought intelligently, and defied the world to find a weak place in his armor. Jack was more subtle and academic; but the father was a towering general. Together, they made a team that must win any battle in which they engaged.

CHAPTER XXI.

JACK MILLER'S LOVE.

There is a general opinion abroad that a man can not do any great, worthy thing while he is making love to a woman. Why that idea should obtain is more than logic or philosophy can reveal. It must have been born of the fact that the first heart affair of adolescent youth is so all-consuming that the fanciful pair forget time, tide, food, and sleep. But a real, grown man makes love best when he is too busy to be sickly sentimental; his love ennobles him and transfigures the most menial tasks into deeds of valor; makes toil seem heroic, and lends unusual competence to his use of plow, pen, or tennis-racket. The woodsman feels like a Caesar, while felling a tree, if only the eyes of his heart's desire are looking on. The fireman never fights the fire fiend so well as when his lady-love is leaning from a window across the street, crying for him to come out of the way of danger. The minister and the politician, who have put away childish things, deliver their messages with more eloquence when they are heard by the pink ears of a sympathtic woman.

Jack Miller was in love. Justa Harris, Marvin's sister, wrought the havoc the first time Jack saw her, after being away for a year. He had not declared himself at the time; but she had interpreted his timid glances aright, and she knew by the rapidity of her pulse that the sensation was altogether pleasant on her part. She was a decided brunette. Although no one called her a beauty, she was attractive and graceful. Her bright smile made up for any lack of "complexion" and she knew how to dress to the best advantage.

She was five years younger than Jack. That accounted for his not having noticed her more as they grew up. She had budded forth in the one short year she was gone, and, during the past two years, she had ripened into the most winsome woman he had ever met. It did not take long for them to come to an understanding; but he was so busy, and the work before him so heavy, that their courtship was a process of months of little moments snatched from the stress of campaign and preparation for the session of the legislature that winter.

Dixie knew of the affection, and approved it most heartily. Here was a chance for one of the family to achieve the ambition of her parents in perpetuation of the old Kentucky stock, and to bless them with a posterity of which they might well be proud. She was sure that Jack was worthy, and there was no question about Justa. Her father and mother were as fine people as had ever lived in the Valley, and there had never been any indication of disease or habit of a vicious nature, with the single exception of Marvin's declension, in any member of the Harris family. Dixie reflected on her own sad lot, and wished Jack and Justa the happiest possible results from their mutual choice.

Jim Miller had a frank talk with Jack when he became aware of the serious nature of his love for Justa.

"My son," he said, during a little respite in their work at the office, "I suspect you are thinking of offering marriage to Justa Harris?"

"Yes, father, I meant to talk it over with you, and I am glad you mentioned it."

"Then, you have not proposed to her?"

"No, sir, I owed it to you to speak to you first."

"Why do you think you owed me that?"

"Well, because I should not like to take such an important step in life without consulting you. I am of age; but our interests are so identical in the work we have undertaken, that I owe it to you to ask your advice and consent to my marriage with any woman. Also, I want the weight of your judgment as to whether my choice is intelligent."

"I certainly appreciate this frankness, son. You could claim your right to marry without consulting me, and I do not know that I would question it. It is true that our great work doubles the bond between us, and I shall be glad to give you any advice I may. Your last remark raises the question of natural selection in marriage; do you not believe in that?"

"No, sir, not altogether. I believe natural selection through the passion of love is all right when, and only when, reason and science make marriage as rational and right to both persons as it is desirable."

"Then, if you were to discover some physical

or mental defect in yourself or Justa, you would not marry?"

"Never! That would be treason to the very cause I am advocating. I am committed to the logic and soundness of our doctrines personally, as well as ethically and theoretically."

"Thank God! I have not lived in vain, and my revenge is sweeter than ever. Dixie has kept her promise, though it has consigned her to the purgatory of a childless existence. Now you prove your sanity by the same test. This is victory!"

"But you do not think there is such reason that I ought not to marry Justa?"

"Only you can answer that, my boy. Are you as pure as you expect her to be when you meet her at Hymen's altar?"

Jack stood up and lifted his hand above his head. "Look, father," he cried, "with my hand lifted to Heaven, I declare unto you that not a single muscle or nerve, not a vein or tissue of my body has ever been stained with a drop of alcohol nor an atom of nicotine; I am unconscious of it if a single germ of any disease has ever impinged on my flesh; I have never conducted myself toward any woman as I would not have any man treat my good mother. Mother's talk to me when Allie died has saved me from all that. I am clean."

As his hand fell, the father sprang up and grasped it in his own.

"I was sure it was so, Jack, but to hear it like that from your lips makes me proud of my son.

Listen. I have carefully investigated my own family, and your mother's as well, and I can assure you that, so far as I am able to discover, the blood is clean for four generations behind you. There is not a case of drunkenness nor inheritable disease to be found in your ancestry that far back. It is up to you to keep the blood clean down the generations to come. This you can do by proper teaching; for, where one generation knows, they will pass the knowledge on to the next. I almost wish I could live a thousand years just to see what can be done in the way of improving one family of the race. Tell your children never to marry into a family that has tainted blood."

"Thank you, father. But tell me what you think of Justa's ancestry?"

"I will have a talk with Mr. Harris, if you wish me to, and let you know."

"That will be the very thing, and how I appreciate your kindness and help."

"I owe you that."

"Perhaps you had better wait a while about talking to him, because I am not ready to marry just yet. I want to get through with the session of the legislature before I think of that; then, I need to get through my study and be admitted to the bar. I might do that after marrying; but that can be settled after the session is over."

"Well, if anything should happen that I should not be able to interview Mr. Harris, Dr. McConnell will serve you as well or perhaps better than I could; I have his promise of that kind of service for any member of my family."

Drury Patterson returned from the East full of enthusiasm and knowledge. He delighted the Club with his graphic accounts of what was being done in the universities and colleges of the North and East, and by the different societies that had been formed to fight the Great Black Plague. He told them of the surprise of educators and doctors when they heard of the real work being done under Senator Miller's leadership. They readily agreed to the measures the Tamalpias Club was urging, and made further suggestions that were acceptable to the club.

It was quite a surprise to him to learn from Dixie of Jack's love affair. He was pleased, however, and, for the first time, showed a little impatience over his own handicap and disability to claim his sweetheart's hand in marriage. If he ever had been jealous, he was jealous now. He felt the call of his heart as she had felt the call of hers. Manhood cried out for its mate. They were in the same car, and they drove along the same road where Dixie had voiced her rebellion a short time before.

"Dixie," he cried, as he brought the car to a sudden stop under the very trees where they had sat before, and grasped her hands in his, "it is the heaviest curse ever put on man. My detectives have learned almost nothing. I am worse than an Ishmaelite; I am like the child-widows of India. They are better off than I; for, although they are forbidden to marry. they may know who their parents are. I am a man, and I feel the emotions, sentiments, ambitions, and those things God has made essential to manhood—companionship, lordship over a home, that kingship that is incomplete without a queen; to know that my life will be lived out in others after me. Oh, it is this that love was designed to accomplish and make perfect! Yet, here I am loving the most adorable woman in the world, sure that my love is returned, and not daring to press the cup I hold in my hands to my lips. O my love, I am almost mad! Why did I not accept your proposition and risk the consequences? Come on, let us go and get the license and marry within the next hour. Will you, my darling?"

"Drury! What are you saying! I never knew you to give way to your feeling like this. Come, be strong; for my sake, be strong."

"Strong? Haven't I been strong? My strength has left me, though. I am a prisoner in the hands of fate. May I not break the bars that hold my spirit captive?"

"No. Justice will come and liberate you in due time. I know it; I am sure of it."

"You will not come with me? You refuse to marry me because I am a nameless waif?"

"Don't Drury! You will kill me. You know it is not that. Did I not prove it the other day when I offered to fly in the face of all our promises, and the objections of my own relatives?"

She broke down, sobbing, and he was sobered at once.

"Forgive me, sweetheart. My God, what have I said!

"Dixie, look up, sweetheart. I was a simpering fool. Look up; I will not lose my head again—it was only the pent up anguish of years—it is over with now, and I am myself again."

"That is more like my big, brave man. I am glad you love me like that, dear man, and I can see now how strong you must have been when I was weak."

"But it was your almost superhuman strength that brought me to my senses. I am surprised at this weakness, and I promise you it shall never master me again."

"I am really glad you did give way a little bit, Drury; for I was beginning to think that either your love was too practical, or that you were more than human in your control of it. We are even. now, and each understands himself and the other better than ever before."

"That is true. And I love you more, if possible."

Then they came back to the land of common mortals, and returned to town, and to their work for others.

Jack's talk with his father awakened his love to unknown depths, and he found himself idealizing its object, and planning his future with regard to her and her happiness. He had never allowed his attention to her, nor his thoughts of her to interfere with his work; but he found it hard to keep from thinking of his plans for the future in which she figured so much. His determination to delay his proposal to her until after the meeting of the legislature was destroyed one holiday. They had gone with a party on a long tramp that took them to Indian Bluff. They carried lunch baskets, and were to gather at the Bluff for dinner. On their way, they gathered pecans. The trees were loaded and the nuts were just beginning to fall. Nearer town, boys and men were thrashing them from the trees and gathering them for market. Jack had a canvas bag thrown over his shoulder, and he and Justa worked vigorously until the bag got so heavy that they hung it on a limb of a tree, and went on to the Bluff in advance of the others.

Both had been there before; but it had never been half as romantic as it was this beautiful fall day. It is a strange fact that a romantic spot has much to do with making the people who visit it romantic. Many a romance is born of environment rather than of inherent worth, taste, or natural affinity. Their romance was already in embryo, but it was the environment, where so many others had culminated. that caused the sturdy young man to throw his determination to the winds. The very inscriptions on the soft rock called for their names to be written with the others.

"It looks such a foolish thing to do, this writing of names on this Bluff, unless one was sure that the names would be coupled like that for life," said Justa. "Look here for instance: 'John Porter Allen and Lucile Altman—7-4-'00.' She married Alfred Pryor, and he is still an old bachelor."

"But here is my sister Allie's name with that of Maxwell Wright. Yes, and here is your brother Marvin's and his wife's. Suppose I carve ours here together."

She averted her gaze; but he could see the blushes she was trying to hide. It was the psychological moment. What real lover could have resisted it? They were sitting on the very edge of the Bluff, and it was impossible to move quickly without endangering life and limb. He slipped his arm around her waist, and drew her to him.

"Justa," he said, "I did not intend to speak to you until I returned from the meeting of the legislature; but I must speak now. I love you—have loved you ever since I came home three years ago, and saw you suddenly sprung from a schoolgirl into a most winsome and lovely young lady. You have given me some reason to believe that my attention has not been hateful to you. Tell me: may I hope to claim you for my wife some day?"

She drew away from his embrace as gently as she could, so that she might look him in the face. She deliberately went over every feature, and looked deep into his eyes. Her voice was steady, but there was a suspicion of moisture in her eyes as she said:

"I am not entirely surprised, Jack, I have known by your actions and manner that you cared for me; therefore I have thought of the possibility of this moment. I did not think it would come so soon; but I must talk plainly with you before I answer your questions. I have watched the progress of your father's noble fight for a worthy revenge for the injury done his family. I am only a girl, but I have been interested in the matter from the first. You have voluntarily taken up the cause, and I am sure you will fight just as hard as your father for these principles. I love you, Jack. Oh, how I love you! I have watched you while you were on the rostrum, and have called you my prince. I have longed to tell you how proud I am of you. But, Jack, dear, you must remember that the Monster came near ruining my brother's home. Ah, you thought I did not know. Nobody told me, but I knew. And I want to know that there are no barriers to our love. I must know."

It was a long speech, and he knew she must have thought over the matter of it many times against this event. Admiration sparkled in his eyes, and his smile told her that he was glad for this frankness.

"You darling girl! My lips have never touched yours, but they must have a kiss from them after they have spoken these brave words. Come, answer my question with a kiss."

"But my simple expression does not satisfy me."

"Ah, I forgot. Justa, I offer you a pure, clean hand. Will you take it? It is as clean as any man ever offered to a woman."

"I believe it, Jack. By a woman's intuition, I have known you are clean. And I am sure your family is all that one could ask. But what about my own? That is what I want to know."

"What! Do you believe for a moment that there is a defect in the blood in your veins? I do not believe it! Come, Justa, give me that kiss, and, with it, your answer that you will be my wife."

"I will give you that if you will promise me that you will demand of my father if he knows any reason why we should not marry."

"Done."

They were warned of the approach of the rest of their party, about an hour later, by the laughter and shouts of the jolly crowd. When the others arrived, the lovers were very innocently throwing rocks into the creek below; but their names were written together on the Bluff.

CHAPTER XXII.

NEW WINE IN OLD BOTTLES.

Winter was just getting a good grip on the Northern country, and, by sending frequent chilling blasts across the Gulf States, was putting forth desperate efforts to make the citizens of the Southwest shiver in acknowledgment of their acceptance of his rule for a few weeks. Norther after norther swept over the prairies, and these were alternated with cold rains and dismal days, unrelieved by the sunshine of which the natives boast so much. Stock was suffering, and the fuel question was serious. Unaccustomed to such weather, the schoolrooms were overheated, and the doors and windows were kept closed in all dwellings and public buildings. The people breathed only vitiated air, and they shrank from the damp outdoor air that would have given them health. Children got their feet damp for want of heavy shoes, and all the malaria that had been stored up in their systems, by the bites of mosquitoes during the fall, became active. No one ever knows what to expect of malarial disorders. There is no other disease as hard to prognosticate, and it renders the system susceptible to the invasion of other germs. Tamalpias escaped the epidemic for the simple reason that the town was in an altitude not infested by mosquitoes, and the atmosphere was dry and full of oxygen. But other towns were filled with sick people, and nurses were in demand. Dixie offered her services under the direction of the House of Healing, and was immediately accepted and detailed to duty in a City Hospital.

Almost without the usual warning of a few advance cases, that dread disease, cerebro-spinal meningitis, became prevalent. The large percentage of fatalities threw the city into a panic, and neighboring towns and cities began to quarantine against them. Doctors offered their services, and Dr. Drury Patterson was among the first to reach the afflicted city and enlist in the work of sanitation and treatment. The scourge increased daily, and other towns and cities began to report cases. Within a month, scores of places were under quarantine, and the whole State became alarmed.

It was at this juncture that the noted Dr. Stephen, who had been studying this particular disease for years, came on the scene to direct the heroic campaign for the stamping out of the plague. Dr. Patterson became such an apt pupil of the expert that he was soon sent to direct the fight in other places. For weeks, he worked almost day and night. He was warned to rest and recuperate; but he laughed at the alarm of friends and associates. The need for his services was so imperative, and the ravages of the disease so great, and so rapid, that he could not rest when he went to bed. Twice, he was tempted, as he had never been tempted before, to take some kind of drug to sustain him against his outrage of nature. Once, an older doctor took a dose of cocaine in his presence, and he noted the almost immediate effect. His tired brain refused to reason out the right or wrong of such an act, and his need of rest and sleep was so desperate that he went behind a prescription-case and poured a dose from a bottle. As he turned to the hydrant and lifted his hand to his mouth, he happened to catch his reflection in a mirror on the wall. Like a flash, his brain awakened, and he stood aghast. What was this he was about to do!

"Fool," he cried, "it has come at last! The awful temptation that I have feared so long has come at last. I might have known it, though. What am I but a 'river-rat' picked up out of the muddy waters of the Mississippi? I might as well take it and go to the Devil. I'll likely go, anyway."

He lifted his hand again, and, again, he saw his image in the glass. This time, his manhood awakened and joined his aroused brain. Then, his will-power buckled on its armor, and called on his manhood to assert itself. Memory, too, came on the scene. Dixie Miller believed in him; she loved him, and, by that, had a claim on him. Her words, "Be strong!" echoed in his ears, and he threw the drug into the lavatory, and turned from the place. The victory gave him strength and self-respect, and he resolved to go to his hotel and get the needed rest. He told the clerk that he was not to be called for any purpose until twelve o'clock the next day. After a refreshing bath, and a few moments of silent meditation, he went to bed.

It was nearly noon when he awakened the next

day. He arose immediately and took a plunge-bath in cold water. Then, he dressed hurriedly, and went down to the office. He refused his mail and ordered a taxicab for a spin before luncheon. As the driver was given no instructions but to "go" for an hour, he drove through parks and beautiful residential sections. But Dr. Patterson was not interested in the scenery. He was examining himself. In the light of a new day, and with his body and mind refreshed, he could not see why he had been so tempted. If he had taken the drug, he would have hated himself forever. He knew he could never have looked in Dixie's face again, and he wondered if the remorse would have driven him to suicide. He shuddered at the very word. Then, the future loomed up before him. There were other days coming. Would he be tempted again, and, if so, would he be weaker than he had been on this occasion? Would there be a mirror to arrest his hand? His thoughts had traveled thus far when the taxicab stopped and he was at the hotel door. As he entered the dining-room, he saw Dixie standing there with mischievous smiles on her beautiful face.

"My, but you are a serious doctor! Run right over your friends and never see them. Come, give an account of yourself."

"Dixie! What on earth brings you here?"

"Haven't I the right to go where I please?" she laughed, mockingly.

"But it is so unexpected."

"Unexpected! Did you not get my letter this morning?"

"No. I refused my mail until I should take a drive."

"So that is it. I was just a little disappointed that you did not meet me at the station. But, go in and lunch; then, we shall have time to talk. I will meet you in the parlor in half an hour."

The epidemic had abated in the first city, and Dixie, relieved from her duty there, had written Drury that she was coming to offer her services in the hospital where he was working. She knew that he was overworked, and she hoped to be able to persuade him to rest.

When he came into the parlor, she was waiting for him.

"Come," she said, "give an account of yourself. I come to insist that you stop and rest, and, when I ask about you, the clerk tells me that you went to your room in the middle of the afternoon yesterday, and gave instructions that you were not to be called until noon today. Then, a bellboy appears, and says that you went out for a drive before lunch. I see that my mission is useless so far as that part is concerned; but, perhaps, I can be of service to somebody who really needs me."

"Somebody who really needs you? That's I."

"You do not look half as needy as I expected to find you."

"But I am more needy than I look. Dixie, I

can not conceal my story from you. I must tell you—I have fallen."

"Fallen! Drury, what in the name of mercy do you mean? Tell me, quickly!" There was anguish and alarm in her voice, and she put her hand on his shoulder and looked into his downcast eyes.

"Not into sin, thank God, but into temptation. And you know what that means to me."

"Oh, how you relieve me! How dare you frighten me that way? But tell me, what was the temptation?"

"I believe I would tell you the innermost secrets of my soul, Dixie. I can not imagine myself keeping things from you. But this is so humiliating to me. Be as kind and merciful as you can."

Then, he told her all; and made it as bad as he could. Even in the telling of it, he saw that it was not quite as bad as he had imagined it.

"So, you see," he finished, "I have some weakness, inherited or otherwise. And that is the thing that I have hoped would not appear in my life."

"Why, you silly man. Did you expect to be able to disobey the laws of nature until your brain and nerves ceased to perform their functions, and then, because a little respite was suggested to you by the habit of another, call it a temptation caused by inherent desire? Did you really desire the drug, or the effect it would produce?"

"No, neither. My body had refused to obey

my will, and I would have welcomed a shock of electricity as much as the drug, if it would have given me back my wasted strength. I simply wanted to go on with my work."

"O my dear, brave, strong man, can't you see that it was inherent manhood and will that saved you, instead of inherent weakness that tempted you?"

"That is a charitable view to take of it."

"No, it isn't. It is the sensible view—the right view. If you could dash that drug from your lips when your mind and body were so thoroughly worn out, you would never think of taking it when you were in a normal condition."

"That is true. What a darling girl you are! And I know now how much I really needed you this morning, surely it was a kind Providence that sent you to me."

"I am glad I came, if only to get you to see yourself in the proper light."

"But it was the memory of you and your words that helped me to assert myself in that trying moment."

Never had Dixie longed to have the right to be with him always, and help him in all his great problems, and lean on his strong arms for life, as she did that day. He was so pure and noble, and she understood him so well that her love for him took on a maternal quality. The sanctity of their affection was forever sealed, and they both recognized that each really needed the other.

"Drury, I have had a strange presentiment for

several days: I am as sure you are going to find your parents, and that they are worthy people, as I am of your presence in this room. I can not tell you how I know it; I haven't dreamed it, nor have I been to a mystic: but I am sure we are to be allowed to have a home all our own, without violating the principles my father is fighting for."

"I wish I was as hopeful. I can not see how it is to come about. I have discharged the detectives, and there is nothing but chance to unveil the past and give me my birthright. God grant that you may be correct, for this life is wearing my heart away."

A messenger boy came to them with an urgent call for Dr. Patterson to come to the hospital, and he told Dixie he would see her that evening, and hurried away.

Dixie was needed, and, the next day, she took up her duties in the hospital. For three weeks, they worked, and fought back the disease until at last it was under complete control. Dr. Patterson's name was printed in the city papers in large black letters, and the citizens petitioned him to locate among them. They offered to build him a sanitarium if he would accept it, and he told them he would take the matter under advisement. Dixie, also, was assured of employment in the very best homes in the city at any price she might ask for her services. No one suspected the attachment of doctor and nurse; for they were too sensible to show their holy affections for each other to a gainsaying world:

Drury and Dixie were still in their hospital work when Dixie received a letter from her mother, saying that Maxwell Wright was married again. It was a shock to the family, because, as the reader knows, Jim Miller had written to the young man, and told him the facts in the case. Maxwell had not believed him, however, and had delayed his interview with Dr. Duncan until he had become enamored of another woman; and everybody knows that Cupid is blind. We do not believe much that we do not want to believe. Maxwell had been married for three months when his mother brought herself to the task of breaking the news to the Millers.

Jessie had several admirers, and one splendid man had offered her his hand in marriage; but she was fully decided that she would never marry. Her one sad experience had proved so disappointing, and her health was not such as she knew a wife's should be; so she declined the offer and was happy in the education of her blind child and what she could do to help her father and brother to make such sorrows as hers fewer. Her grief over the news of Maxwell's marriage was deep. She knew that the new wife was laying herself liable to all that Allie had undergone, and perhaps worse. Time alone would tell.

Dr. McConnell wrote Maxwell a very plain letter in which he warned him of the possible consequences, and how best to guard his wife from the same troubles that had taken Allie to an early grave. His letter was replied to with a curt note that, when his advice was wanted, it would be called for. The Tamalpias Club put

Maxwell Wright's name on their mailing list, and kept him supplied with literature on the subject.

The Christmas holidays found Dixie and Dr. Patterson at home. The minister came in for a few days' rest, and the Club had its final session of the year with all the members present. They had done an immense amount of work during the six months of the Club's existence; Marvin Harris was elected president for the ensuing year. He had become one of the most enthusiastic and effective members, and Jim Miller was glad to have him take his place as the active head of the local organization. Professor Thompson was made secretary, and the membership was increased by the addition of the two doctors who had held aloof until this time.

The Club gave a banquet on New Year's night, and Jessie Tallman presented the minister with a check for a large amount in token of her appreciation of the good work he had done on the lecture platform. The Club gave Jack Miller a gold watch, suitably engraved, and Jim Miller was deeply embarrassed by a speech delivered by Professor Thompson, and the presentation of a loving cup, on which were engraved these words:

"To Our Friend
And Heroic Leader.
SENATOR JAMES R. MILLER.
With the Love and Esteem of Every
Member of the Tamalpias Health Club,
"New wine in old bottles
"Drink hereof and succeed."

When he had time to compose himself and get his voice, Senator Miller replied to the speech of presentation. The one hundred people present had heard him speak on many occasions; but they had never heard him speak as he did then. He opened his heart to them, and told them that his fight was both selfish, and unselfish; selfish in the fact that he had undertaken it as a means of revenge for the life of his child and the sorrows of her twin; unselfish in that it was for the whole race, and not for those he loved, alone. At the close of his impassioned speech, he took up the cup and held it before his face.

"O Cup," he cried, "the Master prayed that a cup might pass from Him. I once prayed that same prayer; but, like the Master, I drank my cup to the dregs, and it was a bitter cup—few know how bitter. To-night I press you to my lips and drink down the draught of love and confidence you contain, and, in the dregs at your bottom, I find the assurance that the venegance I have planned will be wrought even though I die to-morrow. As I sip the sparkling wine of Love that brims you, it becomes a tonic to my ambition, a balm to my wounded soul, a coal of fire to my lips, making them eloquent, a fountain of youth that promises me vigor for years yet unborn in the womb of eternity, a spirit of prophecy that unfolds a future free from our social plague. I take thee to my lips in dedication anew to the emancipation of the imprisoned, the education of the ignorant, and the ostracism of the criminal. Again, I drink of thee. This time, it is the strong wine of confidence, settling on the lees. 'Tis not confidence in me, the man; but confidence, in the righteousness of the cause I represent. I may fail; yea, I fail every day. I may be unworthy; I am. But the cause shall never fail. It is ever worthy. Again, I lift you, O Cup, and see Esteem on your label. That, I hang about the neck of the steed, Purpose, on which I ride into the thick of the fray. And when the fight is done, when I come to hand over the sword to another, may there still be another drop of wine left in you to cheer me across the river into the great Unknown—the drop of consolation, of duty well done. Then my revenge will be complete. Friends, all, I thank you."

If there had been thoughts of lightness and folly, they were dissipated. With his wife and children about him, with his hand hurting from the many grasps of friends, with words of praise in his ears and a great joy in his heart, Senator Miller drove home from the last meeting of the Club he would attend until the great arm of the law should be invoked to assist education in the destruction of the greatest evil that has ever befallen the human race.

CHAPTER XXIII.

THE CYCLONE.

That graphic sentence in the story of Job is the tersest account of a cyclone ever written: "While thy sons and thy daughters were eating and drinking wine in the eldest brother's house, there came a great wind from the wilderness and smote the four corners of the house, and it fell upon the young men and they are dead, yea and the servants also, and I escaped alone to tell thee." It is easy for one who has seen a cyclone to imagine the darkness. the terror, the sudden destruction, and the final downpour of rain when that oriental palace was destroyed by the Prince of the power of the air who was trying to move the patriarch to curse God to his face.

The cyclone season in the Southwest is supposed to begin with the March equinox; but history proves that one may sweep over the country any time from January to July; and the further removed from the cyclone period, the more devastating the storm proves. Every home has its "cyclone cellar" or "storm house," built on the south side or west side of the dwelling. so that the family can get into the underground refuge when the storm is coming, and there will be no danger of the house falling on the door of the place of retreat, because the cyclones always come from the southwest. Most people in that section would as much think of doing without a well of water as without a storm-house.

Tamalpias was out of the general track of cyclones and storms, and many scoffed at the idea of building storm-houses. A few, however, who had lived where the storm is no respector of persons, had large cellars walled with concrete. As year after year passed by and no storm had ever come that gave them just cause to retire to such a covert, they became convinced that their labor and expense had been for naught.

The winter had been very mild and open, and the range grass was already springing up. Early gardens were yielding vegetables, and crops were being planted. One or two pioneers shook their heads and said: "This he-er spell is nawthin' but a weather breeder. I 'member it was jes' sich a spell when that ar twister cum along 'at blowed Jake Ming's house and barn inter kingdom come over in Grayson County, an' 'en went on an' blowed Sidell offen the map. I wouldn't be surprised if the Valley don't get a shakin' up afore Easter."

It was the second day of March, and the warm, bright morning had induced the housewives to put the bedding and spring clothes out to sun Houses were open, chickens were cackling about the barns, men were in the fields, children were at school, and everything seemed tranquil and reminded Doctor McConnell of his favorite poem, "Peaceful Valley." About ten o'clock, the air became murky, making the sun look red like a ball of fire. A deathly stillness fell on all nature, and the noisy hens stopped their singing and cackling, and huddled near their shelter,

Even the negroes, singing at their work, became mute. Only an occasional whinny from a mare, separated from her colt, broke the stillness. The cows came back from the pastures, and the murkiness increased until the sun was entirely hidden. The temperature increased, and those who were watching the change taking place, freely prophesied a "norther." Greedy farmers hung to their plows, anxious to get the most advantage of the season. Women left their bedding and clothes out, thinking it would be a "dry" norther, if one came at all, and the school-teachers only scowled at the gloom that made their rooms almost too dark for the pupils to read.

Dr. Patterson, driving his car like the wind, was going to see a patient living twenty miles north of Tamalpias. He reached a high ridge from which he could see the country for many miles in three directions, and was appalled at the sight that caught his eye. Due south of his position, he could see the great funnel-shaped cloud that was slowly moving in the direction of the quiet valley. Stopping his car, he watched the demon-cloud tearing its way through farms and mesquite bushes. As he looked, he located a ranch-house on Senator Miller's ranch, and, within a moment, it was snatched up, torn to splinters, and was flying in the ever-widening circles of the upper part of that swirling vacuum.

The cyclone was within two miles of Tamalpias, and Dr. Patterson, not heeding the admonition of judgment, turned his machine and was soon racing back. He knew that he would be too late to give warning; but he also reasoned that death and destruction would be left in the path of the storm, and he would be needed. The hills that enclosed the valley made the last three miles of his return very slow. The suction, caused by the passing storm, almost turned his machine over; but he drove on, impelled by the thought that lives were being crushed out right before him. As he came into the valley, a mile north of town, he was disconcerted by the sight he saw, and lost control of his automobile.

Darkness like that of Egypt was being pushed close to the ground in front of the vortex and about it, while following its track, the gray rain-clouds came on like somber mourners dropping their tears on the wreckage of lives and property. The roar was deafening, and the wind was rushing toward the center of the disturbance with such force that the onlooker had to take shelter behind a boulder that jutted out from the hill. The terror was augmented by the incessant display of lightning and the sharp claps of thunder.

As Dr. Patterson felt his machine go into the bank, he cut off the power, and thus escaped being seriously hurt, although the machine was badly wrecked. He did not wait to examine it; for the wind was almost whipping the clothes from his body. Hastily taking refuge behind the friendly boulder, he watched the cloud take a sudden downward swoop and strike the outskirts of Tamalpias. The darkness now blotted out all except the outlines of the tallest buildings; but he could tell that the track lay west of the business section and that the hungry demon would take its heaviest toll from the best residential portion, and the public school-buildings. The churches. too, would be struck. He shivered as he thought of the death-list and the wrecked homes of the people. Even as he shivered, he saw the flying timbers and roofs come up out of the darkness like timbers and boats from a sunken ship, and then be caught by the upper currents and shoot through space in the general direction of the storm. Distinctly. he saw the spire and part of the roof of the Methodist church lifted, as a child might lift the lid from a "Noah's Ark," and go hurtling after the cabins of the negro section first struck. Then. he saw a whole house rise and ride for a few moments before it went to pieces like a soap-bubble. On and on went the death-dealing storm, mowing everything in its path as wheat falls before the mowing-machine.

Drury found himself standing in the torrents of rain, torn between his grief over the disaster, his thankfulness that the Miller house was evidently safe, and his impotence to get to town immediately and be of service in taking care of the wounded. He found his way to the wrecked car, and got his uninjured case. Then. he began to run through the mud, rain, and wind. The creek lay between him and his destination; but it was not yet swollen so much that he could not wade it. Beyond the creek. the road had been built of crushed rock, and his speed increased.

He was among the first to reach the strip of wreckage. and was quick to note that the school-building had barely escaped. With a muttered thanksgiving, he ran on until he came to a large residence that had collapsed and was pitched over the premises in a distorted pile. The trees were either stripped or blown down; but most of the floor of the residence was still intact. He saw a bed still standing on the floor, and, running to it. found the covers undisturbed. He had waited at this very bedside the night before until a young life had been put into the hands of a pair of happy young parents. He had uncanny feelings as he approached it now; for he was sure that mother and baby must be dead. As he reached out his hand to lay back the cover, the quilt was pushed aside, and the pale, but smiling face of the mother appeared. On her arm lay the baby, sleeping. protected from the rain by the pillow that had been beneath its mother's head. Drury drew back awestruck; but the mother laughed nervously, and said:

"O Doctor, I prayed to God, and He heard me and delivered me and my child from the 'destruction that wasteth at noonday,' according to His promise."

"Where is your husband?"

"He picked up my invalid mother and carried her to the storm-house. I hope he got there safe. The house must have fallen on the door, so he could not come back to me."

"No, the house fell the other way; but a tree

has fallen on the storm-house, and I am sure they are safe. I will see."

He called through the air-stack, and found that both were safe in the shelter; he assured the husband of the safety of his wife and child, and hastened to get help to release the prisoners, and to carry the helpless to shelter.

At the church-site, he found several persons who had been on their way home, and had taken shelter there. The building, a substantial frame, had been blown from its foundation, and the walls had fallen when the roof had been blown off. Part of the refugees had perished, and others were wounded and maimed. The stone church was a block away, and had been just outside the track of the cyclone. It was thrown open for use as an emergency hospital, and there they carried the injured and the dead. Boards and mattresses were laid on top of the pews along the aisles, and doctors and women bound up cuts and bruises; held dying heads, amputated crushed limbs, and restored those who had been shocked into blessed unconsciousness.

Dixie was on the scene as quickly as she could get her father's car out of the garage and run it the short mile that intervened between the suburban home and the devastated portion of the beautiful city-of-the-valley. She was the only trained nurse there, and there were not doctors enough to take care of the many injured; so she put her training and observation into practice, and was soon sewing up cuts, setting broken bones, and stanching bleeding wounds like a real doctor. Marvin Harris had not been in the storm, but was severely hurt by a falling wall while rescuing an old man, who was pinned down by some timbers. He was carried in on a stretcher, and Dixie waited on him. When she had bandaged his broken arm, and had sewed up the gash in his scalp, he told her that she was a great woman, and he wished from his heart that Dr. Patterson's parentage would be discovered so they would marry and be happy as they deserved to be. It was the final word that made them better friends than she had ever hoped they could be.

Word was brought to Drury, again and again, that his cottage had been blown from the foundation and wrecked; but he refused to stop his work of relief to look after his own fortunes. All through the day, the doctors worked, and into the night. He was the youngest doctor among them, and he insisted on staying at the church all night. Part of the injured ones had been removed to near-by residences; but it would require the constant presence of a skilled doctor at the church. Dixie, and many of the men and women stayed also. Three of the most seriously injured died during the night, and others were thrown into fever and second shock.

The rain had ceased and the sky was clear when the morning broke. The air was crisp and cold, and it was hard to realize what had happened within twenty-four hours. One could stand at the railroad and look at the track of the storm, one hundred yards wide and a mile long, and not a building could be seen standing upright. Many were missing altogether, and some were scattered for blocks. The rescuing party had recovered all the bodies except two, and they had been burned in the wreckage of the home they had lived in for many years. Other fires would have added to the terror of it all, if it had not been for the pelting rain that had quenched many a blaze.

The night-watchers were relieved at sunrise by those who had taken some rest, and Drury and Dixie walked to the ruins of his home, three blocks from the church. It had been a beautiful cottage; now, it lay a crumpled, twisted, broken mass of white and green splinters.

"Oh, it is just too bad, isn't it?" cried Dixie.

"It is bad, all right; but think of those who have lost more. I can rebuild all this, but some of them have lost parents, and children, and companions, and others have lost homes they will never be able to rebuild. Oh, what a terrible time it has been!"

"Yes, I thought the plague, last winter, was bad enough, but this is the most suffering I ever saw."

They entered the lawn over the fence that was flat on the ground, and found their way through the tangled trees and shrubbery to the broken walls of the cottage. Drury crawled through a broken window and called to Dixie to come after him. It was the room in which Mrs. Patterson had died, and the bed on which she had lain was crushed under the broken planks and the bricks and mortar of a fallen chimney. Some of the bricks had struck the desk and caved the top in. Pictures were gone from the walls, and the door to a closet was wrenched from its hinges. A trunk was showing through the open door, and Drury pulled it out.

"This is my mother's trunk," he said. "It is about to fall to pieces. I suspect I had better take it and the desk outside, before the walls fall on them and finish their destruction."

Suiting his actions to his words, he began to drag the trunk across the uneven floor, when it literally fell to pieces. Its contents were a surprise to both of them. A complete baby's wardrobe was exposed, and it was so dainty and elaborate that Dixie gave a little cry of surprise as she gathered it up in her arms. Little red shoes and bootees, lace caps and embroidered flannels, white dresses and silk stockings that would delight any mother on earth were there in abundance. Drury was pulling out of the mass other finery—that of a woman. Such clothes as he had never seen Mrs. Patterson wear, the clothes of a grand lady, and with them jewelry and trinkets that were strange to him. Then, a few things that he recognized as the rather plain clothes of his foster-mother.

Dixie's womanly intuition told her these were the baby-garments the woman had talked of in her delirium—the garments she had coveted on that mysterious trip up the river. She was holding in her arms the clothes that loving mother-hands had made for this man she loved. Then, the thought came that perhaps they were marked. She dropped the lot and bent over them, examining a skirt.

"Oh, look!" she cried, "look, Drury, look! "Here is the name—'McPherson!'"

"What's that!" And Drury dropped the clothes he held so reverently, and took the skirt from the hands of the excited girl.

"McPherson." He turned the garment over and around, as if in search of information. "McPherson," he said again. "I never heard them speak of any one of that name. What can it mean?"

"O can't you understand, Drury? These are your clothes, and that is your name—Drury McPherson!"

"No, surely that can not be."

"But it is, I am sure." Then she flew to the dresses he had dropped and began to examine the wardrobe.

"Yes, here it is again, as plain as can be, and in the same writing with black indelible ink, 'McPherson,' and these are your mother's—your own mother's clothes. O Drury, I am so excited I do not know what to do. We have found out your name!"

"Not too fast, little girl. We must have more than circumstantial evidence or surmises. I must know positively who I am and what I am. Let us keep this to ourselves until I know certainly that I have a right to the name, and that it is more worthy than the one I now bear."

He turned to drag the desk from its corner.

Dumping it over on its side to knock the dust and mortar from it, he received a second shock. The whole top, crushed by the bricks, fell to the floor, and revealed a secret drawer that was hidden by the moulding that finished the top of the desk. Numerous papers fluttered across the floor, and a book tumbled out. Dixie was arranging the clothes in a suitable stack, and did not notice what had happened. Drury did not call her attention to his find at once, for he wanted to know what it was first. Opening the book, he read on the title page:

"To relieve my burdened conscience I have here set down the events that have been burned into my memory like letters of fire. Not being allowed to talk to Mr. Patterson about them, and thinking of them continually has almost upset my mind, but I must tell these things, if only to a book. Should this chronicle ever be found, it is to be turned over to Drury Patterson, my foster-child. And I hope it will be the means of his happiness, even though he hate me for the part I have taken in the tragedy of his life."

His nervousness was so great, and the groan that escaped his lips was so audible, that Dixie heard it and was at his side in a moment.

"O Dixie, I am about to know the truth of my birth and parentage, and I am so nervous. Won't you read it to me, dear?" And he handed her the book.

Her excitement was as great as his, but it was the excitement of joy and relief. His was still full of anxiety.

"Come," she said, after glancing through the book; "it will take an hour to read this; let us go to your office."

So they gathered up the papers, having put away the clothes, and went to Drury's office to read the story both had been wanting to know for so long.

CHAPTER XXIV.

MRS. PATTERSON'S JOURNAL.

As Drury and Dixie entered the office and passed to Drury's private room, both knew they were about to come face to face with an hour pregnant with possibilities and revelations that would affect their happiness for a lifetime. Drury was more nervous than ever, and his impatience to know the facts was overtopped only by his half-acknowledged fear that the facts would not be entirely welcome. He would prefer to remain a nameless waif, doomed to a life of lonely service, rather than to find that he was the child of undesirable parents. Dixie pushed back the light-brown hair from his forehead, and kissed him there as she said brightly:

"Cheer up, Drury, dear. You look more as if I was going to read a sentence of death than a birthright. Smile for me, just once, and then I will read."

"How can I smile, when it may be worse than a death-warrant? Go on and read it, and perhaps I shall smile then."

"But, O Drury! Your sunny smile always helped others. So many times you used to say 'cheer up, the worst is yet to come,' and the worst perplexed boy or girl would smile. Come, I won't begin until you smile. There, that is better. Now, I can read." Then, she began:

"How am I to begin this story that has been

like a millstone about my neck for so many years? I have never been a good writer, even of letters, and shrink from setting down here the things that, written by an able pen, might be called a story indeed. I suspect it would be better for me to go back to my childhood and tell the whole thing. I was born of poor parents, named Warren, in an humble home in the State of North Carolina. When I was nine years old, the family moved to Mississippi, where I grew to womanhood. While poor, my parents were devout Christians, and honest, patriotic citizens. My sister, Martha, married a cotton-buyer who lived in Memphis, and I visited her several times. It was on one of these visits that I met John Patterson. I loved him from the very start. None of my relatives had ever used whiskey, but his drink did not appear to hurt him. I rather liked the effect it had on him. He was more courtly and gallant when he was drinking, and he never appeared to be intoxicated, or drunk, as some would call it. My brother, Basil, seriously objected to my engagement to Mr. Patterson, and aroused the opposition of my sister and my parents. That only increased my determination to marry him, and we were married by a minister, at his residence. Mr. Patterson was always kind to me, and we lived in better style than I had been used to. We went to Georgia and visited his people for a time; then, we returned to Memphis, where Mr. Patterson had some kind of business. He never told me what it was. Then, my baby came. He was a pretty boy, and I was happy. I idolized him, and Mr. Patterson could not go to his work for sitting and holding the baby. He was so changed in his manners and appearance, and he did not drink for two months. We named the baby John Gorman, after Mr. Patterson and my father. When little Jack, as his father nick-named him, was two months old, we went to New Orleans to attend Mardi Gras. I could not enjoy the festivities for spending the time on my baby. I would sit in the hotel and study the way other babies' clothes were made, and wish I knew how to make them like that for my baby. An inordinate desire to see him decked out in finery possessed me, and I bought a lot of goods and laces, which I expected to have made for him when I returned to Memphis.

"At last, the day came for our return. The excursion was over; but a great many people had remained in the city as we had done, and the boat we embarked on was crowded with passengers. Our stateroom was near that of a man and his wife who had a baby just the age of Jack, and the two looked so much alike that the ladies remarked about it several times. Even Mrs. McPherson, for that was the lady's name, said to me that she had never seen two babies look so much alike. I did not think so, for I thought my baby looked more robust than the other. The McPherson baby was named Drury, and they called him Du. It was not his looks that I admired so much, but the clothes he wore. I never had seen such embroidery and dainty baby-things in my life. Every time she came out of her stateroom, she had a different dress on little Du. That made me jealous, and I did not keep my baby in the salon more than I was compelled to. I coveted those dresses. God only knows how much I coveted them.

"That night, I could not sleep, for I was planning to dress my baby so that he would outshine any baby in Memphis. And I was going to buy a buggy for him that was made of willow wickerwork. It was after midnight, and the monotonous thud of the engines was about to succeed in hypnotizing me into a light sleep, when I heard some one running overhead. Then the clang of the bell, and the whistle began to blow in short blasts. The cry of 'Fire' rang out from the salon, and pistols began their popping reports to awaken the passengers.

"I called to Mr. Patterson, who was sleeping in the upper birth, and hastily threw on a wrapper, and, catching up my baby, ran out into the cabin. The fire was in the rear end of the boat, and I could see the flames eating through the walls not twenty feet away. My first thought was to save my trunk with all the pretty goods I had bought, and I told Mr. Patterson to get it and have it ready to throw overboard, if we were not able to land before the boat sank. The cabin was filling with excited passengers, and I saw the McPhersons emerge from their stateroom with the baby in his nightgown. Mrs. McPherson saw John dragging our trunk, and she begged her husband to get theirs. I remember thinking at the time that we were the only ones trying to save our trunks.

"The fire was lighing up the river, and we could see that we were still quite a distance from the east shore, toward which the boat was headed. All the passengers, very naturally, gathered on the side of the boat, in spite of the attempt of the officers to make them stay back from the guard-rail. The crowd was so large that their weight made the boat run lopsided, and the engineer must have lost control of the steering device; for we soon found the vessel turned with her prow down-stream. Then, the fire drove the men from the engine-room, and we were adrift on the burning boat. The panic was fearful. Men leaped into the water and swam toward shore, women screamed, and babies cried. Children got lost from parents, and pandemonium seemed to be turned loose. I clung to Mr. Patterson and told him to hang to the trunk until he could crowd to the rail and throw it overboard. The McPhersons were just in front of us, and he had her small steamer-trunk on his shoulder.

"I shall not attempt to describe the cursing of the wicked, the prayers of the religious, nor the offers of the rich to any one who would save them. The boats were lowered from the upper decks of the steamer, and a great fight ensued, in which men were pushed into the water, and women were lifted over the rail to men below, who put them into the boats. Once the boats were loaded, they were rowed quickly to the shore and deposited the refugees. As they came hurrying back to get others, there was a great crush to get to the side of the boat, which had been anchored to keep her from drifting down the stream. I was almost squeezed to death, and Mrs. McPherson cried with pain. Just then, the guard-rail broke and we were all thrown into the water. I suppose it was my grasping for something to hold to that caused me to drop my baby as I fell. Then, I held to a man's coat, and some one was holding to my gown. Oh, I can not set it all down here! I lived almost an eternity there in the water. I had been able to get a breath or two of air by holding on to the man, but the struggling mass kept my head under the water part of the time. I was on the surface now, and my face blistered in the heat as we drifted by the burning end of the boat, which had again swung down-stream. Just then, I saw a rope thrown from a row-boat, and I seized it with both hands. At almost the same instant, a babe, wrapped in a heavy wool blanket, floated into my very arms. Instinctively, I caught hold of the blanket, and we were both taken into the boat, and I was afraid I would be drowned before we could be brought to shore. But we were landed safely. The night was balmy, and the men built a fire of driftwood. My heart beat fast as I undid the blanket to see what kind of a baby I had in my arms, and then I almost screamed aloud as I saw that it was little Drury McPherson."

Dixie's voice choked, and she stopped reading to recover. Drury was sitting low down in his chair with both hands shoved into his trouser pockets. He was looking as stolid as an Indian, and Dixie knew he was gripping himself with all his will power.

"Go on, read it," he said, without a movement of any kind. And she resumed the story.

"My first impulse was to find his mother. Then, the wicked thought came that perhaps she was dead. My baby was gone and I never expected to see it again—if she was not found, I would claim her baby, and I would find his trunk and have all those fine clothes. I think I was crazy that night, and perhaps I have been from then until now. Sometimes I think it is the solution of it all. Little Du was in his nightrobe—a plain little one, such as my baby wore. I sat there by the fire and cried over the loss of little Jack until the morning began to break. Somehow, I had little thought of Mr. Patterson, and when I did think of him, I was sure he was safe. And he was, for he came hunting among the rescued people for me. He took it for granted that it was our baby in my arms, and told me he had landed the trunk on a sand-bar half a mile below where we were rescued. He confiscated a skiff and we rowed down to the place to get the trunk. Men were recovering what bodies they could, and they had several laid out on the sand. I felt weak and sick, and, when we walked among the dead and I came to the body of a lady whom I recognized as Mrs McPherson, even before I saw her face, I fell in a swoon.

"When I opened my eyes again, I was lying

under a tree on the high bank overlooking the sand-bar. John and a strange lady were with me, and I saw the baby, wrapped in his blanket, lying beside me. The trunk I prized so highly was also near. I was weak from the exposure and strain, but I begged Mr. Patterson to take me back to the shore where they were recovering property and bodies. He refused at first, but finally yielded to my entreaties. I wanted to be sure whether my baby was recovered or not, and still I was afraid to tell him what had happened. Mr. McPherson was not on the bar, and we heard a man say that he was injured.

"In looking about, I saw the small steamer trunk, with the letters, 'S. C. McP.', on the end, and I knew it was hers, and that it contained those fine clothes. What ever possessed me to covet those clothes like that? I seemed like another person, and the loss of my own baby did not seem at all real. If only I could have this baby and his fine clothes, and could get away where no one would ever take him from me, I would be satisfied. I called Mr. Patterson aside and told him what had happened. He refused to believe it until he saw the smiling face of the baby as it awakened from its sleep. He sat down there on the sand and sobbed like a schoolboy, and refused to enter into my scheme. But I was desperate, and I am sure now that the fright and exposure gave me hysteria, for I flew into a tantrum, and when he saw that I was all but crazy, he gave up and went for the trunk. But he told me that, if they claimed it, he would see that they got it and the baby too.

"We went back to the tree where my trunk was, and I succeeded in transferring all the nice things I wanted, to it. Then, when John was gone to secure a place for us to stay until we could get transportation, I dragged the small trunk down the bank and dumped it into the river.

"O reader, whoever you may be, do not judge me too harshly. I was demented, and my sin has been repented of ten thousand times. My sin? Which was the greater sin: to steal the live child and his clothes, or to so quickly transfer my love from my own flesh and blood to the child I argued a kind Providence had thrust into my arms? Was it a sin of my heart in coveting the finery? Or was it due to the disordered condition of my mind? I do not know. But I do know it was wrong, and yet I never had the courage to try to right the wrong. Mr. Patterson would have corrected the matter any time during the first year, had he not been afraid it would send me to the madhouse. And it would have done just that. After that, he came to love the child in his own way, and then he began to fear that, if we were found out, he would be convicted of kidnapping. That settled the matter, and we began to travel and never went back to that section of the country.

"But to resume my story: Mr. Patterson hired a man to drive us to a town five miles down the river that day. I suspect he would have taken the next boat, but I wanted to attend the funeral of the wreck victims the next day. He did everything he could to prevent my going, but I got a lady to take me in her surrey. I left the babe with John. The bodies were all to be buried in a country graveyard four miles north of Branden, because of their rapid decomposition.

"Thirty-three graves were open, and there were said to be thirty-five bodies—two babes would be buried with their mothers. I saw Mr. McPherson there with his head all bandaged, and his arm in a sling. He asked for his wife's casket to be opened, and I crept near. O my God! There lay my baby Jack, by the side of the dead mother, whose child I had rescued. I screamed out, but there were so many screaming that I was unnoticed. They had found the baby, and the poor injured father had easily mistaken it for his own. Again, I lost consciousness, and, when I recovered, the funeral was over, and it was time to drive back.

"I waited until we were on the boat, bound for home, to tell Mr. Patterson what had happened at the cemetery. He was angry with me for keeping up the deception; but I was more determined than ever to keep the baby. It is so easy to charge God with helping us to do wrong. I consoled myself with the thought that God wanted me to have that baby, or He never would have cast him into my arms in that miraculous way. The child never would know the difference, and it was not long until I loved him as my own.

"Mr. Patterson must have found out something about Mr. McPherson, for he became restless and wanted to move. We went to St. Louis and stayed there three years. Then, we went to Cuba, and to California. He took to drinking harder, and I was scared when he would come home drunk; for it was then he would make dire threats of what he would do to me if I ever told anyone about the boy. We called him Drury, because I could not bring myself to call him Jack.

"At last the news came to us that Mr. Patterson's parents were dead, and that he was to have the homestead at Tamalpias. That suited us both, for we were sure no one would ever find out about our sin over there."

Here the writing had ceased, and evidently a long period of time had passed until she had turned two or three pages and begun again.

"Drury, my dear boy," she wrote, "I have just come from putting some flowers on Mr. Patterson's grave. It has been a sad time for me. I wish I could bring myself to tell you of my crime in stealing you away from your father. When I saw your fear that you would some day be like John Patterson, I came very near telling you all about it. But my sin has made me such a coward that I could not bear to face you with the story. I hope you will find this book. I am going to leave a note telling you how to open the secret drawer to this desk, which my father gave me, if I do not die too suddenly. If I do not do that, I shall trust to the same Providence that put you in my arms to reveal it all to you in

His own good time and way. And when you do find out, I plead with you to love me just a little, and to forgive me for what I have done.

"I am sure I will not live much longer. This secret is a cancer that is gnawing my heart out. You are now a great, good man, and you do not need me any longer. I just want to die. I am leaving some papers in this same drawer, which I found in your mother's trunk——"

Dixie stopped reading, for Drury had leaped to his feet and snatched the papers from her lap. His stoicism was gone, and his excitement was shaking him so that he could scarcely read the yellowed documents. One was a marriage certificate attesting to the marriage of Stephen Carlisle McPherson to Narcissa Scott, and the ceremony had been performed by the Rev. T. C. Teasdale, at Memphis, Tennessee. Another was a genealogy of Narcissa Scott's family for five generations preceding her, and there was the date of the birth of Drury Scott McPherson, at Savannah, Georgia, and the date was the one Mrs. Patterson had taught him to observe as the anniversary of his birth.

As he read this last paper, Dixie cried out: "O Drury, you have the blood of two Governors in your veins, and of several of the greatest men the South has ever produced! Isn't it fine!" And she danced about the floor like a child on Christmas morning.

There was another paper written by Mrs. Patterson, which contained minute directions for finding the grave of his mother on the banks of the Mississippi River. When he had finished them all, he laid them on the table, and sat down with his face in his hands. Who, that has not experienced them, can describe the emotions that filled the soul of this man, who had found his mother, but found her dead for twenty-five years; had found his name, and the probable right to marry the woman he loved; and yet, who must fulfil his resolution to bring to his future father-in-law the undoubted proof of his ancestry on both sides of his family. He was worn out with watching, shaken with grief, proud of what he had learned, torn with his love for the beautiful woman who was sharing everything with him, and filled with his plans for finding his father, if that father was still alive.

He arose from his chair with a real smile on his face, and reached his arms for Dixie. She went to him with a happy laugh.

"Think of it, darling," he said, "only a few short weeks, and I shall have the joy of calling you my wife! I just know my father's family must be all right; but I am going to find out. I will start tomorrow."

"God bless you, dear Drury, my fine, strong man; I shall not eat or sleep until I hear from you. You must wire me the first moment you learn the truth. Oh, I love my dear Mr. McPherson!"

"That sounds queer. Let us still call it Patterson until I complete my title."

"But we must tell dear old Dr. McConnell, and my father!"

"Yes, we shall tell them, they have a right to know; but the others must wait a short while. I shall want your father to hear it from me, though, and I shall go by the Capitol and tell him the story. I shall take these records with me, and I want you to go to the cottage and get the clothing that must have been my mother's, and take care of it for me."

"I will, and the little dresses she made for you that caused Mrs. Patterson to covet them, and then to steal you."

Then they went and told Dr. McConnell together, and he became excited.

"I have known all the time that there was something wrong. I said you were not a Patterson. You may have looked like their baby when you were little; but anybody with half sense would know that you are of better stock than that of John Patterson and his wife.

"Yes, go. Go and find your father, and bring him here that we may know him. Bring him here to attend the wedding, for it must be right away."

"Yes, Dixie has promised to marry me the very day I return with a clean pedigree," and Drury kissed the hand he held.

CHAPTER XXV.

DR. DRURY'S QUEST.

Drury found it impossible to get away for a week, on account of the serious injuries of so many people. All the doctors were kept busy night and day caring for the stricken citizens. Senator Miller and Jack came home by the first train after hearing the news, and the former was happy over Drury's good fortune in finding out so much about his parents.

The long week passed, finally, and Drury boarded the train that would speed him on his way to his mother's grave, and to—what?

He went to New Orleans, then up the river to the little village of Braden. He had heard of the overflow a few months previous, and was fearful that the village had been washed away. A fellow passenger set his mind at rest on the matter before his journey was half done, by telling him that the town was safe, and that the cemetery of which he spoke, was on a ridge above highwater mark.

At the Braden Hotel, he was directed to a livery-stable, where he secured a team and driver, and was soon on his way to the burying-ground. It was late afternoon, and the mid-March sun shone warmly in that southern clime. Everywhere, the signs of spring were abundant. and the farmers were working in the upspringing crops. The driver was an old man, and he remembered the wrecking and burning of the Katie

Malone as though it had been yesterday. Then, he launched into his oft-repeated version of the accident, and how he had helped to dig the graves of the victims. Drury did not ask him about his mother's grave. He was afraid to do that for fear it would be found neglected, or not found at all.

On their arrival at the cemetery, he was surprised to find it one of the best-kept graveyards he had ever seen. The ground was clear of grass and weeds, and the walks were covered with gravel, and bordered with large shells from the river. White stakes and posts marked the blocks and lots, and each one was numbered with black figures.

"Yes," replied his driver, in answer to his exclamation of amazement, "we are proud of our cemetery. Old Mr. Hughes has the books, and he can tell you who is buried in each and every grave, and when they were buried. Come on over here and I'll show you where the people are laid that were drowned that time the Katie Malone went down."

He led Drury to one side, and pointed out several graves that were unmarked save by a white board with a number neatly painted on it. A few of the graves indicated had small slabs of marble; but one, farther on, had a tall shaft of gray granite over it.

"Whose is that well-kept grave with the granite monument?" asked Drury, as they came to the line of graves.

"That is the grave of a woman and child. They

put the child in her arms; a little baby a month or two old. Her husband was almost killed when the rail broke from the crowd surging against it. He comes here every year and covers the grave with flowers. I did know where he comes from, but I have forgotten; I can't remember things like I used to. Now here is where they—"

But Drury had pushed past him, and was hurrying to the grave that he was sure held the body of his own mother. Coming to it, he read the inscription:

"Narcissa and Drury,
Wife and Infant
Son of
S. C. McPherson.
Died
April—— 18——"

There was a short poem and a quotation of Scripture. That was all. The plants and flowers were fresh-worked, and there were some pot-plants that had recently been placed there. The plot was surrounded by a curb of granite, and on this Drury knelt and wept. Nor were his tears from the shallow fountain of sentiment; they were from the deepest emotions of his manly soul. Here his father had shed tears for his child as well as for his young wife. It was as though he wept at his own grave.

The driver drew near, and his human sympathy made the tears run over his seamed face. He wiped his face with a rough hand, and asked:

"Mister, or, Doctor, I believe you told us you was, is it some of your kinfolks that we laid here twenty-five years ago?"

"My mother," he managed to answer, and the word relieved him.

"Why, I guess you're mistaken, Doctor. She only had one child, and that was buried with her. I remember that because there were two others buried the same day, and none of them had but the one child."

"But it was another baby they buried with my mother. I was rescued from that boat by another woman, and her baby was mistaken for me."

"I reckon you will have a hard time making Judge McPherson believe that. He saw his child, and identified it, and he will think you have come along trying to get his money with a story like that."

"That is all right, my good man. You may drive me back to the town, now, if you please. And it would be just as well if you keep all this to yourself until I find my father."

At the hotel, he asked to see the register, and the clerk was able to turn to the very place where Judge McPherson had last registered. His name was written in a bold hand, and the address given was Atlanta, Georgia. Drury learned that the sexton of the cemetery was paid a stipulated sum to keep Mrs. McPherson's grave, and that the Judge had come each year, until the last two, to see it. He had written to know about the grave, and had explained his absence by saying that his duties as Judge had prevented his annual trip.

Again Drury, who had lived more in twenty-five years than many men live in seventy, took up his journey in quest of a parentage that would not only give him a father, but that would enable him to take unto himself a wife whom he had loved for eight long years. It was night when he reached the city, and he went to a hotel and to bed. He was weary and needed the rest, and he wanted to meet his father when he was fresh and presentable. The night did wonders for him. He felt like a new man when he came from his morning bath, and partook of a wholesome breakfast. From a city directory, he learned his father's address, and was starting to take a car when he reflected that it would be better to telephone and see if he was at home. Some one replied to his call, and said that the Judge was out just then, but would be at home at eleven o'clock.

The time passed slowly for the son who had never looked into his father's face since an infant. Tiring of the hotel, he concluded to see the city, and called a taxicab. He had an hour and a half, and he told the driver to take him over the prettiest part of the city slowly enough that he could see the points of interest. As every Atlanta driver does under such orders, he was taken first to that famous boulevard, Peach-Tree Street. He found himself repeating the words of the Queen of Sheba: "The half has not been told," for it is a wonderful sight to the visitor. Then, he was taken through parks and drives that awakened his interest to such a pitch that he was alarmed when he opened his watch and found that it was just eleven. Giving the driver instruction to drive to the address where his father lived, he leaned back and began to wonder what the parental residence would be like. It is a strange fact that he had not once tried to imagine how his father would look. When he thought of him, he pictured him sitting in the crowded graveyard with his head bandaged and his arm in a sling.

The taxicab stopped before a beautiful stone residence with a tile roof. The grounds were spacious and well kept, and two pretty fountains were in full flow. It was almost a fairyland to this man of the hills and plains of the West.

A negro man, in olive-green livery, answered his ring, and he saw at once that a card was expected. Fortunately, he had a few cards, and he quickly gave the footman one, and waited until he returned and bowed him into the hall.

"Come this way. The Judge is in the library," said the servant.

At the library door, he bowed low and stepped aside for Drury to enter. At a table, in the center of the luxuriant room, sat a man not more than fifty years old. His hair was almost white, his clean-shaven face was noble, kind, and yet full of sedateness and sternness that made him look venerable. The keen, deep-set eyes, and the well-molded nose denoted the student, while his large size and good color bespoke robust health. He was on his feet in a moment. "How do you do, Doctor—" glancing at the card—"Doctor Patterson. Have a seat."

"Thank you, Judge McPherson."

"I believe I have not met you before. Are you a stranger in the city, Doctor?"

"I arrived last night."

"I take it that you have come to see me on professional business?"

"Yes, and no. I want to ask you about the accident to the Katie Malone, on the Mississippi River, twenty-five years ago. I understand you were on the boat that night?"

"I was. But you are too young a man to have been there also. Perhaps some of your relatives were lost that night?"

"They were. My mother was drowned that night. Did you not lose your wife then?"

"Yes, and my baby, too. What was your mother's name?"

Drury was somewhat confused by this unexpected question; but he avoided it for the time.

"Judge McPherson," he asked, "did it ever occur to you that there might have been a mistake in the identification of the babies that were found on the sand-bar the next morning?"

"What do you mean? What can you mean?"

"Just this: there was another couple on that boat, named Patterson. They had a child the same age as yours, and both children were said to look alike. The child that was buried with your wife was dressed in a little night-robe such as almost any child would wear. You were hurt, and easily took it for granted that the babe was your own. Is it not possible that the other couple lost their child and found yours alive and claimed it?"

"Possible, my dear sir, but not at all probable. I can see how a scheme to present me with an heir at this late day could be worked out along these lines; but it would take more than a plausible story to convince me."

"I think I have such evidence, Judge. I have here a number of things. Allow me to say that I am the child that was rescued that night."

"The Patterson child? I remember them; and I also remember that Mrs. Patterson came to the funeral, and how she screamed when she looked into the casket and saw mother and babe together."

"No wonder she screamed; for, according to her written confession, which I have here, she was looking at her own child instead of yours."

"What is that? She claims to have substituted her child for mine?"

"No, she claims that it was accident that substituted, or exchanged, the children, and, then, she deliberately stole me from you."

"Stole you! She claims that you are my child!"

"That is it, exactly."

"God in heaven, help me. What is the man saying!"

"Hear me out, Judge. If what Mrs. Patterson makes written confession is true, and if her dying words were true, you are my father, I am your son that has been mourned as dead for a quarter of a century."

"Give me the confession—the evidence. It seems like a tale from 'Alice-in-Wonderland.'"

He took the book from Drury's hands, and began to read. Slowly at first, then with quick, nervous hands, he turned the leaves of the record. More than once, he let the book fall to the table and looked across at the young doctor. The further he read, the oftener he looked, and Drury could see that conviction was being borne in on him that the story was true. As he finished the reading, Drury handed over a small package. Judge McPherson undid it, and there lay before him a dainty baby-dress.

"Ah, I know that dress. I watched Narcissa ply her needle many an evening while she made that. Oh, I am sure it is all true! And you are my little Du that——"

He could say no more, but walked around the table, and the two men went into each other's arms.

A moment later, a woman stood in the doorway, exclaiming: "Stephen, what is the matter? Oh, I beg your pardon, I did not know I was intruding."

"Come back, Addie," called the elder man. "Come here. I want to introduce to you my son, Doctor McPherson; my wife, son."

"Your son! I do not understand."

"Neither could I, until I read the confession of the woman who stole him the day Narcissa was buried. It was not my child that was buried with her; it was the child of a Mrs. Patterson, and this is my own child, my son, come to me a full-fledged doctor, and a good one, I hope."

Then, the household was notified, and Drury found himself surrounded by two sisters and three brothers. His oldest half-sister was a beautiful young lady of about twenty summers, which must have been happy ones, judging by her sweet face. There was a boy eighteen, a girl fifteen, another boy eleven, and one eight.

Dinner, which Mrs. McPherson had come to the library to announce, was served, and the servants seemed as glad of the dramatic appearance of the new son as were any of the family.

"You haven't told us, Drury, are you married?" asked the Judge, in the midst of the meal.

"No sir; but I here and now give you all an invitation to my wedding to Miss Dixie Miller within a month."

"My, how sudden!" exclaimed Mazie.

"No, not sudden, Sister. I have wanted to marry her for many years."

"And why haven't you?" asked the father.

"That is a long story. It has to do with the whole question of heredity and physical fitness to marry."

"I see. You could not marry her when you thought yourself the child of John Patterson; then, you would not marry her until you knew your ancestry was all right. Is that it?"

"Your powers of perception are very keen, Father."

"Well, I am glad to tell you that there never

was cleaner blood than that which flows in your veins, my son."

"Next to that which establishes my relationship to this fine family, that is the best piece of information I have received for many a day. I could never ask Senator Miller's daughter to be my wife without the knowledge that I was offering to her a clean hand and a pure body. She must never have the trouble, nor bring to her parents the sorrow, caused by the marriage of her beautiful twin sisters to men who were unfit for marriage at all."

Then, he told them of his life and his friends; about his work, and that of the great man whose daughter he was to marry; of Tamalpias, and its Health Club, the principles of which he had helped to mold; of Dixie Miller, the beautiful girl who had become a trained nurse because of his supposed parentage; of the two compaigns, and the hoped-for success of father and son, who were then in the legislature fighting for an unselfish revenge against the Monster that had ruined the lives of their loved ones.

So much was Judge McPherson impressed with his capable son that he gave a luncheon in his honor the next evening, and invited a few of the city's best physicians. Drury was surprised and embarrassed by being told by one of the best surgeons in all the South that the work and lectures of the little company at Tamalpias were already attracting the attention of educators and doctors throughout the country, and it was freely prophesied that the work of this generation in that line was going to accomplish more for the race than anything that had been done during the past five hundred years.

Drury found his father an honored and wealthy citizen of the city, and his cultured family very popular in the best circles of society. For a week he was kept busy attending receptions and social functions, and he was proud of being introduced by his lovely sister as "my doctor-brother, whom we have just found."

As soon as he could get away from them, the first afternoon, he sent Dixie a telegram, which read:

"News too good to wire. Am writing. Will be at home next week, and will expect you to keep your promise right away.

"(Signed) Drury Scott McPherson."

He wanted the whole family to return with him for the wedding festivities; but it was impossible for any of them to go, save his father and his oldest sister, Mazie. Judge McPherson told him of his mother, and proposed to take him to see her people on their way West. Drury was overjoyed with the prospect, and could hardly wait for the journey to begin. They left Atlanta on Tuesday, and arrived at the City of Roses on Thursday. Judge McPherson had wired the Scotts he was coming, but had not told them of Drury, and the party was met at the station by a venerable man, whose flowing white hair and fine face made one think of Henry Ward Beecher, and by a young man, who was introduced as Dr. Walter Scott. Drury was introduced simply as Dr. McPherson, and explanations were reserved for a time when the family would be together.

The old gentleman proved to be Drury's grandfather, and the doctor, his uncle. His grandfather was a retired minister, and his grandmother, who was still living, was a dear old lady of the old type, which is fast disappearing. There were aunts and cousins by the score; for it was a family that "claimed kin" as far as the least relationship could be traced. He was shown pictures of two ancestors that had been governors and of one that had been a major in the war of the sixties.

A rare treat awaited him. His father had shown him photographs of his mother; but her parents had an oil painting of her that had been made just before her marriage to his father. He stood before it for hours, and wished he could have seen her. She was so different from Mrs. Patterson that he knew what he had missed by her death. He was astonished above measure when his grandfather led him to the painting, just before his departure, and made him a present of it.

"You are taking your father home to see you married. Take this picture, and show it to your bride. Tell her your mother was one of the fairest flowers the death-angel ever plucked from earth. You can see she was beautiful; but she was as pure and good as she was beautiful."

"O Grandfather," he stammered. "You embarrass me by your kindness. I would rather have that picture than any legacy in the world. I thank you a thousand times, and I know Dixie will be so glad."

Dr. Scott was proud of his nephew and tried to persuade him to locate in The City of Roses, and enter into practice with him; but Drury told him it was his ambition to become a great surgeon, and that he intended going to Germany for a course of study.

Promising to return to see them soon, and to bring his bride, Drury, with his father and sister, left them on Saturday and turned his face toward home and Dixie.

CHAPTER XXVI.

REALIZED DREAMS.

Up to the time of the death of Allie Miller and the suicide of Maury Tallman, Tamalpias had had only one real sensation. That was when the big hotel, which had been built to accommodate the horsemen and the gamblers that followed the races, had burned, and two of the guests had lost their lives. Since the troubles of the Miller family had begun to develop, there had been much to disturb the quiet life of the town. The scarlet fever and diphtheria epidemics, John Patterson's tragic death, the campaigns Jim Miller had made, and the cyclone, following in rapid succession, had prepared the inhabitants for almost anything. However, the return of the young doctor they all knew and loved, accompanied by his father and sister, and the announcement that he was not the child of the Pattersons, but the child of one of the first citizens of Georgia, threw the citizens into an excitement that put a stop to all work and traffic for several days. Some stood about and shook their heads, and one said:

"You can never know what to expect these days. I can hardly believe it is so."

"Pshaw!" answered a neighbor. "I aint' a bit surprised; I allus did know Drury was better'n them Pattersons. He never did look like either one of 'em."

"Well, I don't care what name he goes by," observed another; "he is a fine doctor, and they ain't another un in all this country what could a' saved my little Bob when he had scarlet fever. I like him just as well with one name as with another."

Old Rilla was staying with Jessie Tallman, and she could not get over the great news.

"Now, Miss Jessie," she said again, "does I understan' that Mis' Patterson, she done tuk de trunk an' de baby an' lit out afore dey could catch her? Yessum, an' she lef' her own chile layin' dar in de arms o' dat lady, jes' so? Umph? An' he sho' nuff ain't de chile o' no drunker, is he, Miss Jessie? An' dat gran' gemmen is he pa! Lawdy, but I is glad; kase, now den, Miss Dixie kin mahry him, kain't she, Miss Jessie?"

"Yes, Rilla, she is going to marry him Easter Sunday—a week from next Sunday."

"Yessum. Ain't dat mighty sudden like, Miss Jessie?"

"You must remember they have been waiting to get married for six years, Rilla."

"Den, why for didn't dey?"

"Because he wanted to know that he was the child of good parents, and fit to marry, first."

"Fitten? Dr. Patterson—no, I mean Dr. Mc— What is it, Miss Jessie?"

"McPherson."

"Yessum, McPhersum. Dr. McPhersum ain't never been anything but fitten. He ain't never run 'round lak other men. He's allus been fitten."

"What does 'fitten' mean, Mama?" asked Little Jim, as he felt of a mechanical toy Drury had brought him from Atlanta.

"That is Rilla's way of saying 'good,' darling."

"Well, she is right. Uncle Drury is good, isn't he, Mama?"

Dixie had taught him to call Drury uncle, and he always said it. His teacher had succeeded in teaching him many things that children of his age did not know. His association with grown folks continually had given him a sagacity that was unusual, and he wanted to know the reason for everything. He loved to go to the cemetery and place flowers on his father's grave, and he talked much about the time when he would go where Papa was and be able to see him.

The legislature was still in session, and there was strong liability that the Governor would call an extra session immediately. One or two of Jim Miller's bills had passed, and the others were in fair prospect of being enacted into law; but it was doubtful that the chief executive would approve the one that required certificates from physicians before a marriage license could be obtained.

Senator Miller and Jack went home to be at the wedding on Easter. It was a simple affair in the church. Neither the bride or bridegroom wanted anything elaborate, and their wishes were respected, even to the lack of excessive decoration. Jim Miller gave away the bride and Drury approached the altar on the arm of his father. Jack Miller and Mazie McPherson did the honors, and the same minister that had married the twins took the vows.

Jack and Justa were tempted to move up their date, and embark on the sea of matrimony with Drury and Dixie; but they decided to wait until May-day, as they had already planned.

There was no happier man in the Valley than Dr. McConnell. He was proud of his partner, and he was proud of Dixie. He thought Judge McPherson and Jim Miller the two grandest men he had ever met, and he told them so. His gift to the couple was a promise to have the cottage rebuilt at his expense, and have it ready for them on their return from Europe.

Jim Miller and Judge McPherson found a natural affinity for each other from the first, and the two families soon felt that they had known each other always. Mazie and Jessie were together much, and the former got a vision of life that she had never had before. She saw the righteousness of the great cause Senator Miller was giving his life to, and she returned home an advocate of his high principles.

Dixie's dream of touring the world with Drury came true. They left the dear little town of their childhood on an April day, when the whole earth was full of blossoms and life, and they sailed from New York with a merry party of tourists. It was early in the season, but they wanted to spend some time in England and France before going to the far East. Jessie had told Dixie of things to look up, and they sometimes felt sad as they stood where Maury Tallman had stood with his bride, full of hope and happiness.

Then, they went to Egypt, and on to Palestine, and through Suez Canal, to the Orient. It was a great trip for the young people, who had come through so much sorrow and so many disappointments. As they neared the shores of their native land, their hearts swelled with pride for the best country on the globe. It was September when their ship entered the Golden Gate and anchored in the Bay of San Francisco. It was the grandest sight they had seen. Nowhere in all the world can one find more to excite wonder and admiration; nowhere can one see more at a glance: Oakland and Berkeley on the east, the Ferry Building and the towers and hills of 'Frisco on the west, Yerba Buena and Alcatras Islands, like gems rising out of the Bay; Mt. Tamalpias standing like a guardian over the way to the sea, while boats and ships plow the waters, and cargoes from Orient and Occident are coming and going.

They visited the navy-yard, at Mare Island, and went to see the wizard, Burbank, at Santa Rosa; through the mighty groves of eucalyptus-trees, up to Mt. Shasta; down the San Joaquin Valley, and over to Santa Clara to see the famous big trees; to the Yosemite, and to St. Catalina Island; then to Long Beach, and the orange-groves that never fail.

"It is like the king of the feast who said of the wine Jesus had made: 'You have reserved the best until the last,'" observed Dixie, as they sat in the Sunken Gardens, at Pasadena.

"Yes, I believe that Italian Prince was right who said that Americans were fools to go gadding to Europe simply for sightseeing. He said there was nothing in Europe to compare with our scenery, and I agree with him."

"I have been thinking how dull it would be unless one had some one along to share it with him. I would not want to make the trip without you."

"Nor I without you, Dixie. But I am longing to get back to our dear old Southland. How I would love to smell a magnolia, or a Cape jasmine!"

"You just said that to make me homesick, you bad boy. I would like to hear the band play 'Dixie' once more, too."

"And you said that in retaliation! But we shall be at home one week from today, if nothing happens."

CHAPTER XXVII.

JIM MILLER'S REVENGE.

Again, the large bell at Villa Maria was announcing early mass, and, again, the children of Tamalpias were scampering hither and thither hunting Easter eggs in the dewy grass. But the pool on Senator Miller's ranch was as quiet as the grave of Allie Miller when the old negro nurse, Rilla, entered the bath-house and sat down on the steps. She was as sentimental as she was superstitious, and was now muttering to herself:

"I'se lived mos' long enuff, now, and I'se jes' waitin' fer de good Lawd to lemme come on home. But I had to come down he'er once mo' and see de ol' pool whar dem angel-twins use ter come a-bavin' ebery mawnin'. An' des think, it war ten y'ars ago dey come home from dat big school back yander some'ers, and tuk to playing like ducks in dis spring. An' 'en it was nine y'ars ago dis bery mawin' dat dey was adippin' and aswimmin' in dat watah des like watah-fowls. Now whar is dey? Miss Allie done daid, an' Miss Jessie de bes', lovin'est widder in de world, and got dat li'l blind Jim what knows mo' in a minit dan lots o' white chillen what's got two good eyes, an' he ain't got narry un. He's gwine to be like his big father what kilt himse'f, on'y he's gwine to hab too much sense to kill hese'f. So, dey's nobody lef' ter swim in you, purty, cl'ar watah, 'cep' when dey's comp'ny come from de city to see Marse Miller, er when Marse Jack is ter home ag'in.

"Des well quit yer singing', mister mocking bird, lessen you go out to de simitry an' sing in de cedar what grows whar Miss Allie's buried, kase nobody's gwine to hear you."

"What's all that you are saying, Aunt Rilla?"

"Who dat?" cried the old woman, leaping up. "'Fo' God, Marse Jim, you done scart me plum to def."

"I did not know you were here. I came to look at the pool once more. I haven't seen it for nearly two years."

"That's what I come down he'er for the same thing, Marse Jim. Its bein' Easter, I jes' nat'ly had ter come."

"It is a pretty pool."

"Yes, sah; yes, sah; but not half as purty as it used to be when y'all's baby-twins used to come down he-er ebery mawnin' and play about in it like fishes."

Senator Miller turned away quickly; for that was what had brought him to the spot. He, too, was sentimental, and had wandered out this fine morning to see the pool he had built to please the twins. But he did not want to discuss the matter with anybody, not even with his wife. He was going to take his family—wife, children, and grandchildren—to the cemetery before going to church. They always went there on Easter morning. But he had come on this little stroll that he might allow his memory to turn to his

had gathered at the pavilion in the center of the yard, Jim Miller lifted his voice so that all could hear.

"Friends," he said, "we have come here this Easter morning, according to a most beautiful custom, to remember our dead, and to place upon their graves these white lilies, emblems of the resurrection. Death is no respecter of persons, and reaps from all our homes; it loves a shining mark, and many of these graves hold the bodies of the sweetest children, the most beautiful women, and the best men that ever lived. But a bow, bright with the promise of a glorious immortality, arches this sacred spot, and fills the future with the hope that you and I shall see our dead again.

"You, my good friends, know why I and mine are here today. My public life has unavoidably revealed my deep bereavement, and I have been compelled to tell why I have been aroused to the fight for the race. The monster crime of our boasted civilization—social sin—dug those two graves yonder, and many more like them on this plot of ground. Seven years ago, I learned the truth; since that time, I have spared neither time nor money, energy nor influence, that I might in some measure avenge the wrongs inflicted on my children; the death of one and the widowhood of another; the sightless eyes of this bright child, and the aching heart of the mother of my children.

"You have helped me in the fight, and you, as much as I, are the beneficiaries of the victory that has been won. But the victory is sweet to me, sweeter than I ever dreamed it would be. Give me that child, Dr. McPherson, and your sweet girl, Jack. Look at these, my friends. I am so intoxicated with the wine of revenge that I dare hold up these, my grandchildren, and tell you that they have come into the world under the conditions I have urged so strongly among you. Thank God, there are pure men and pure, high-minded boys in this country, and on them rests the responsibility of the coming generations.

"Mollie," he said, turning to his weeping wife, as he brushed the tears from his own noble face. "I am almost ready to say that our loss has been great gain. We lost a daughter, but we have been able to save a thousand women what she suffered; we have mourned, but now we are comforted. Jessie, my daughter, you are avenged. Your sacrifice has been great, but your help in the work of enlightenment has been incalculable. Dr. McConnell, you are a grand old veteran, and will soon go to your reward. You, too, have paid toll to the Great Black Plague; but you have had your part in this battle that has emancipated the slaves of lust. Soon, you will hear the call: 'Come up higher; you have been faithful, have rule over much.' Among the younger men here, no one deserves greater praise than Dr. McPherson. Drury, my son, no man ever won his bride more bravely, and none deserved the woman he got more than you deserve the last girl I had to give away.

"O friends, this hour pays a hundred-fold for all that has gone before it. Let us keep up the fight until all men shall be compelled to stay entirely out of the wild oats patch, or live in it. Jack, my boy, you have kept your promise so well; but there is plenty to be done yet. Never let up as long as there is such a thing as the Great Black Plague in America.

"It will be fitting to have this dear old minister, who has seen more than half the graves here filled up, lead us in prayer and pronounce a benediction."

This the reverend man did, and the company turned from the city of the dead and went out among the happy children, and to the stone church, where the music and Easter bonnets were as exquisite as they were on that first day we met Jim Miller's girls.